Welcome to the world
of Sydney Harbour Hospital

(or *SHH…* for short—
because secrets never stay hidden for long!)

Looking out over cosmopolitan Sydney Harbour, Australia's premier teaching hospital is a hive of round-the-clock activity—with a *very* active hospital grapevine.

With the most renowned (and gorgeous!) doctors in Sydney working side by side, professional and sensual tensions run sky-high—there's *always* plenty of romantic rumours to gossip about…

Who's been kissing who in the on-call room? What's going on between legendary heart surgeon Finn Kennedy and tough-talking A&E doctor Evie Lockheart? And what's wrong with Finn?

Find out in this enthralling new eight-book continuity from Medical Romance™—indulge yourself with eight helpings of romance, emotion and gripping medical drama!

Sydney Harbour Hospital
From saving lives to sizzling seduction,
these doctors are the very best!

Sydney Harbour Hospital

Sexy surgeons, dedicated doctors,
scandalous secrets, on-call dramas...

Welcome to the world of Sydney Harbour Hospital
(or *SHH...* for short—
because secrets never stay hidden for long!)

New nurse Lily got caught up in the hotbed of hospital gossip in
SYDNEY HARBOUR HOSPITAL: LILY'S SCANDAL
by Marion Lennox

And gorgeous paediatrician Teo came to single mum Zoe's rescue in
SYDNEY HARBOUR HOSPITAL: ZOE'S BABY
by Alison Roberts

Then sexy Sicilian playboy Luca finally met his match in
SYDNEY HARBOUR HOSPITAL: LUCA'S BAD GIRL
by Amy Andrews

And Hayley opened Tom's eyes to love in
SYDNEY HARBOUR HOSPITAL: TOM'S REDEMPTION
by Fiona Lowe

Heiress Lexi learned to put the past behind her in
SYDNEY HARBOUR HOSPITAL: LEXI'S SECRET
by Melanie Milburne

Last month adventurer Charlie helped shy Bella fulfil her dreams—
and find love on the way!
SYDNEY HARBOUR HOSPITAL: BELLA'S WISHLIST
by Emily Forbes

Single mum Emily gives no-strings-attached surgeon Marco
a reason to stay this month:
SYDNEY HARBOUR HOSPITAL: MARCO'S TEMPTATION
by Fiona McArthur

And finally join us next month for the final instalment
of this fabulous series as Ava and James realise their marriage
really is worth saving in
SYDNEY HARBOUR HOSPITAL: AVA'S RE-AWAKENING
by Carol Marinelli

And not forgetting *Sydney Harbour Hospital's* legendary heart
surgeon Finn Kennedy. This brooding maverick keeps his women
on hospital rotation... But can new doc Evie Lockheart unlock
the secrets to his guarded heart? Find out in this enthralling new
eight-book continuity from Mills & Boon® Medical Romance™.

A collection impossible to resist!

These books are also available in ebook format
from www.millsandboon.co.uk

SYDNEY HARBOUR HOSPITAL: MARCO'S TEMPTATION

BY
FIONA McARTHUR

First published in Great Britain 2012
by Mills & Boon, an imprint of Harlequin (UK) Limited.
Large Print edition 2013
Harlequin (UK) Limited, Eton House,
18-24 Paradise Road, Richmond, Surrey TW9 1SR

© Harlequin Books S.A. 2012

Special thanks and acknowledgement are given
to Fiona McArthur for her contribution to the
Sydney Harbour Hospital series

ISBN: 978 0 263 23079 6

Harlequin (UK) policy is to use papers that are natural, renewable and recyclable products and made from wood grown in sustainable forests. The logging and manufacturing process conform to the legal environmental regulations of the country of origin.

Printed and bound in Great Britain
by CPI Antony Rowe, Chippenham, Wiltshire

A mother to five sons, **Fiona McArthur** is an Australian midwife who loves to write. Medical Romance™ gives Fiona the scope to write about all the wonderful aspects of adventure, romance, medicine and midwifery that she feels so passionate about—as well as an excuse to travel! Now that her boys are older, Fiona and her husband Ian are off to meet new people, see new places, and have wonderful adventures.

Fiona's website is at www.fionamcarthur.com

Also by Fiona McArthur:

FALLING FOR THE SHEIKH SHE SHOULDN'T
SURVIVAL GUIDE TO DATING YOUR BOSS
HARRY ST CLAIR: ROGUE OR DOCTOR?
MIDWIFE, MOTHER…ITALIAN'S WIFE*
MIDWIFE IN THE FAMILY WAY*
THE MIDWIFE AND THE MILLIONAIRE
MIDWIFE IN A MILLION

Lyrebird Lake Maternity

These books are also available in eBook format from www.millsandboon.co.uk

To Flo, who went above and beyond
to help me do justice to Marco.

Looking forward to more journeys with glee, Fi.
xx

CHAPTER ONE

MARCO D'ARVELLO paused in a pool of sunlight on the suspended walkway and watched the boats in Sydney Harbour. Not your usual view from a hospital corridor. He hoped to do more than just observe this country before he had to leave, but once this last client was seen he was booked up with all the surgery he could manage before he moved on.

That was how he liked it.

His attention returned to the consultant's referral in his hand. 'Foetal urinary obstruction.' Should be a fairly simple scope and shunt, he mused as he pushed open the door to his temporary rooms. The lack of waiting-room chairs meant his patients had to wait in his office. It wasn't really ideal but the view was worth it.

'*Buongiorno*, Marlise.'

His borrowed secretary blushed. 'Good morning, Dr D'Arvello.'

'Please, you must call me Marco.' He perched on the edge of her desk, oblivious to the flutter he caused, and peered across at her computer screen. 'Has Miss Cooper arrived?'

Marlise sucked in her stomach and pointed one manicured figure at the screen. 'Yes. About ten minutes ago.'

'*Bene.*' No time for dawdling. He hated tardiness himself.

When Marco strode through his door the view of the harbour and his nebulous thoughts of probable intra-uterine surgery paled into the background as Miss Cooper's smooth bob swung towards him.

Bellissima! The sun danced on the molten highlights of her hair like the boats on the waves outside, and emerald eyes, direct and calm against his suddenly dazed scrutiny, stared back at him as he crossed the room and held out his hand.

She shifted the big handbag on her lap and a smaller one as well, and stood up. Two bags? He forgot the bags, focussed on the slender hand in front of his, and remembered to breathe. Her fingers were cool and firm and he forced himself to let them slide from his grasp.

Her face. Serenity, wisdom, yet vulnerable? How could that be? She was older than he had expected, perhaps late twenties, maybe early thirties, the perfect age, and where she hid her baby he did not know, but she certainly had that gorgeous pregnant glow about her.

Marco consulted his notes to give time to assemble his scattered thoughts but he only grew more confused. Twenty-six weeks' gestation?

'You don't look very…um…pregnant.' Hell. Say something unprofessional, why don't you?

Emily Cooper blinked. They hadn't told her the new hotshot O and G consultant exuded raw magnetism like a roving gypsy king. Hair too long, too dark, windswept, and gorgeous velvety brown eyes that made her want to melt into the hospital carpet.

Her have another baby? If she could make her mouth work it'd better not laugh. 'I'm not pregnant.' Once was enough, she thought.

She hadn't had a relationship in who knew how long. Her shaky legs suggested she sit, but once safely down she felt like a sex-starved midget with him towering over her. But it wasn't only that, it was the whole broad-shouldered, 'span your waist with his big hands' thing that was happening. A random 'if I was going to have sex it would have to be with someone like him' thought that made her blink. Not her usual fantasy—that was more in line with 'wish I could sleep the clock around'.

Thankfully he stepped around the desk and she savoured the relief of increased space between them.

'But you're here for in-utero surgery…yes?' Such a delicious Italian accent. Emily tasted the sound like chocolate on her tongue.

Marco stared at the paper in his hand. He could easily grasp the most complicated sequences of micro-surgery but this he could not fathom. Not only the sudden misbehaviour of his rampant sex hormones but the concept of being inexplicably glad Miss Cooper was not pregnant. It was all very strange. Perhaps with the desk between them his brain would function.

Before she could answer, the sound of footsteps and a young woman appeared hurriedly at the door. Things fell quickly into place.

'How could you start without me, Mum?'

Fool. He felt like smacking his forehead. But excellent. He could see the similarities as the still barely pregnant-looking daughter came into his office with a mulish look to her rosebud mouth as she took the other handbag from her mother.

'My apologies, Miss Cooper.' He smiled and held out his hand. 'I am Marco D'Arvello.' Reluctantly the young woman shook his hand. 'We have yet to begin.' He extended his apology to Emily. 'And forgive me, too, Mrs Cooper.'

The daughter glowered and glanced at her mother. 'We're both Miss Cooper. Mum's Emily and I'm Annie. Illegitimacy runs in the family.'

Emily. Marco struggled to keep his face neutral when, in fact, he wanted to stand between this little virago and her poor mother. He was slightly relieved to see that Emily had ignored her daughter's outburst. Truly, family dynamics were none of his business, he didn't want them to ever be his business, so why did he feel so discomfited by what was going on here?

He forced himself to concentrate on the younger woman. 'Then let us discuss your child, Annie.' He gestured to the other chair. 'Please, be seated and we will begin.'

Emily held back the sigh along with the need to fan her face. Maybe she could disappear into the carpet until the air-conditioner cooled her cheeks. Why did her daughter's newly emergent evil twin have to appear here? The secretive one she didn't recognise. It was okay. Her daughter was emotional, scared for her baby and angry with the world since Gran had died.

Emily was pretty angry about that herself but really she just longed for the delightful girl child Annie had been up until the last two months.

Illegitimacy runs in the family. Cringeworthy at the very least. No chance of sex with him now.

The thought brought a reluctant whisper of

ironic amusement and suddenly she didn't feel the need to sink into that scratchy hospital carpet; she could focus.

Which was lucky because they'd carried on without her.

'There are three types of foetal surgery. One we do only with a needle. Another is the opposite, and similar to a Caesarean section where we work directly on the anesthetised foetus, which we remove from the uterus and then return.'

Incredible what they could do. Emily watched his face. So intense and obviously passionate about something he knew so well. She couldn't imagine the tension in an operating theatre for such a procedure. It sounded easy. Too easy for reality.

'The risks of premature labour are greatest the larger the incision into the uterus, of course, until sometimes it is better to wait to deliver the baby and perform the surgery ex utero.'

Annie was chewing her lip. 'So can we wait for my baby?'

'Those cases depend on the foetal problem. Your baby is twenty-six weeks old, too young for the risk of premature labour or delivery, too old to be left much longer before damage cannot be reversed, and so we move on to the next alternative.'

He picked up the large envelope of ultrasounds and crossed to the light projector on the wall to clip up the dark images.

They all moved to fan around the light source. 'Foetoscopy would be my preferred option in your case. Or Fetendo—like the child's game—because the instruments are controlled while watching a screen and are less than a pencil width in diameter.'

'Neat.'

'*Si.*' He smiled, the room lit up, and Emily felt like grabbing her sunglasses from her bag.

Probably just because working permanent nights made you sensitive to light.

Marco pointed with one longer finger. 'Your baby has a narrowing of the neck of the bladder.' He circled the darkness of the bladder on the film. 'In simple terms, the door to releasing urine from the bladder has closed almost completely and the kidneys are swelling with the retained fluid. I would have wished to perform this surgery at least four weeks ago for maximum protection of your baby's kidneys.'

Emily felt she had to explain. 'We've only just found out about my daughter's pregnancy. This is the first scan she's had. It's all been a bit of a shock.'

Understatement. And not just the pregnancy. Disbelief that her daughter had fallen into the same circumstances as herself had paled when they'd discovered Annie's baby was at risk.

Emily's fierce protective instinct embraced

this tiny new member of their family whole-heartedly because already she loved this little dark gnome on the ultrasound films.

'*Si*. So we will schedule surgery as soon as possible. I believe the repair can be achieved by foetoscopy under ultrasound imaging.'

He smiled at Annie. 'The instruments are fine and require a very small incision.' He glanced at them both under dark brows. 'Tomorrow?'

'Tomorrow?' Annie's squeak made Emily's hand slip across the distance between them to squeeze her daughter's cold fingers.

'It's okay. Better have it done as soon as possible for baby.' She looked at this man they were entrusting Annie and her baby's future to.

His strong profile and unwavering eyes somehow imbued the confidence she needed that these risks were worth it. 'Do you think much damage has been done to baby's kidneys already?'

He tactfully shrugged his broad shoulders and

their eyes met and held. She could feel his compassion. His understanding of her fear.

They both glanced at Annie. 'We wait. It will be difficult to tell until after the operation. Hopefully the amniotic fluid volume will increase as the bladder is allowed to empty. That will be a good sign.'

He looked at them both. 'And in a few months, after the birth, there will be tests to give a true indication.'

Marco watched the young woman to see if she realised there was still doubt on the final outcome. They did not intrude on the dark sea of the foetal world without good reason. Annie's eyes, glistening green like her mother's, were glued to his face. 'So the procedure is safe for my baby?'

Ah. She began to comprehend and this part of it he could reassure her on. 'I have performed foetoscopies many times, and while you must be aware of the risks—your own anesthetic, your baby's analgesia, which we administer to prevent the procedure causing pain, and the risk of premature labour I spoke about before—to not perform this surgery would ensure a poor quality of life for your child, with extremely damaged kidneys.'

Annie gulped and nodded. 'Yes. I see.'

Perhaps he had been too blunt? 'I do not say these things to frighten you, but for you to know I believe this needs to be done, and as soon as possible.' He touched Annie's shoulder reassuringly. 'Do you understand?'

Annie glanced at her mother and nodded her head 'Okay. But I don't want to know any more. Let's just get it over with, then.'

'*Si.*' He moved to the door and they both stood up. 'I will arrange this now.' He glanced at the notes in his hand. 'I have your mobile phone number and will confirm the time Annie is to arrive tomorrow morning. You live together?'

'Yes.' Emily nodded. 'How long will she be in hospital?'

He pursed those sinfully chiselled lips and Emily diverted her glance quickly away to watch her daughter. 'The risk of premature birth is still present so at least forty-eight hours. My secretary will arrange for Annie to have an injection to help mature her baby's lungs should premature labour occur. This will be repeated tomorrow before surgery. If we have to open the uterus, her stay in hospital would be almost a week.'

Emily glanced back, careful to avoid looking at his face, stared instead at his collar and nodded. 'Thank you, Doctor.'

Marco looked at Annie. 'You are sure you have no other questions?' All mulishness and bravado had fallen away and Annie looked what she was. An apprehensive young woman scared for her baby.

'As long as my baby will be all right, Doctor?'

'Please, call me Marco. And your baby's wellness is our goal. *Bene*. I will see you tomorrow.'

Annie stiffened her shoulders and lifted her chin. 'Tomorrow.' She nodded, resolute. Now he admired her. No doubt her courage came from her mother. 'Thank you, Marco.'

The mother, Emily, just smiled and followed her daughter. No doubt this woman's whole life revolved around the girl, which would explain why there was an imbalance of power for the teenage years. He watched them walk away and readjusted his thinking. The daughter wasn't too bad. Just stressed. And if his child had required what hers did, he'd be stressed too.

He tried not to think about the mother. Because he really wanted to think about her. A lot.

But she did not look the kind of woman to

have an affair, a liaison for just a month, while he worked in Sydney.

Unfortunately, after such brief exposure, her image was burned into his brain. Miss Cooper. Emily. Green eyes and vulnerable wisdom.

Emily went to work that night, like she had so many nights before over the last sixteen years, though times had changed in the last decade as she had progressed in her career. Now she was in charge of the ward at night, instead of being the junior nurse.

She could have risen higher but she chose night work because night duty meant the only person who suffered was her.

Because Gran, dear Gran, the only one in her family who had unconditionally loved her, had supported her, and in the past had minded the sleeping Annie while Emily worked.

Gran was gone now, Annie was certainly old

enough not to be minded, and though Emily had almost come to terms with having a grandchild, she hadn't really come to terms with the fact her daughter had had unprotected sex at sixteen.

Would that have happened if she hadn't worked nights? Who knew? After all those conversations!

The ward was quiet so far—unlike her mind. She set the scales beside the prepared bed for the impending transfer from a regional hospital and pulled the BP machine close to hand for when their patient arrived. Her thoughts roamed as she taped the name badge to the bed.

The new patient was under Marco D'Arvello as well. So they had an influx of foetal surgery now?

She shook her head.

'Is something wrong?' Lily, her colleague and friend, touched her arm and Emily gathered herself.

'No. I'm thinking about earlier today.'

'So how was Annie's appointment and the mysterious Dr D'Arvello?' Lily had recently met and fallen in love with the man of her dreams, a plastic surgeon, and she was keen for everyone else to be as happy as her. 'I hear he's a heart-breaker.'

Um. Gorgeous? Emily could feel the warmth creep up her neck. At least the dimness of night duty was good for hiding blushes. 'He seemed very nice. You tell me what you think when he comes to see the new admission.'

She didn't want to think about her visceral reaction at his office. 'Naturally it would have been better if Annie had had the ultrasound earlier. But I didn't find out until last week. How history repeats itself.'

Her young friend shook her head emphatically. 'From where I'm standing, history did not repeat itself. From what you've told me, your parents treated you with coldness and contempt. This time it's different. When you found out you didn't hesitate to support Annie. You're there for her and she knows it. Even if she won't tell you who the father is.'

Emily chewed her lip. 'She says it's over and he's not interested. I'm not pushing. But her life as a child will be gone. And now her baby might be sick.'

Lily might be young but she hadn't had an easy childhood. She was tough and could work anywhere in the hospital, used to be an agency nurse, but wards were vying for her shifts because she was so versatile. Luckily she loved Maternity and Theatres.

Lily knew how strong a woman could be if she had to be. 'Lots of girls manage beautifully. Even with sick babies. I survived. You survived. You took it on with your head high. She'll survive. And if her baby is like you two, she'll be tough, too.'

Emily breathed deeply. She would love to believe that. She squeezed her friend's shoulder. 'Thanks. I'm sorry. I shouldn't bring my worries to work.'

Lily shook her head emphatically. 'And where else do you go to unload? I'm glad to be here for you. Which reminds me, we should have coffee this week, and Evie wants to come.'

'And that's another thing.' Emily brushed her hair out of her eyes. 'Annie wants a baby shower.'

'Stop beating yourself up. You do a great job. It's been a hard year with your gran and now Annie's pregnancy.'

They both looked up at the sound of an approaching wheel chair. 'I'll try. Looks like our patient is here.'

The woman in the chair looked even younger

than Annie and both women shared a sympathetic glance.

'Hello, there, June, is it?' Emily smiled down at the scared young woman. 'I hear you're having twins?'

June nodded. 'That's what the doctor said. Now I don't feel so bad I look like the side of a house.' Her smile dropped a little as her bravado faltered. 'My babies are going to be all right. Aren't they?'

'We'll be doing everything we can to stop your contractions and as my friend here is fond of saying, babies are tough little creatures.'

The porter wheeled her into the prepared room. June moved carefully, and her large abdomen became more obvious when she moved. She stopped for a moment and breathed through the next contraction and Emily rested her hand on June's belly to feel the muscles harden. 'The tightenings seemed strong. You're managing well with them.'

June breathed out a big sigh when the contraction had passed. 'I did one of those calming birth weekends. My friend's mum teaches them and it really does help.'

'I've heard they're excellent. Must get the number from you for my daughter later.' Emily helped June balance on the scales. 'With luck we'll weigh you and get you into bed and sitting up high before the next one.'

June swayed on the scales and she whistled at the numbers. 'I never knew babies were so heavy.'

Emily wrote down the weight with a smile. 'A lot of your tummy is fluid, not just babies.'

June glanced across at Emily. 'The ultrasound said one baby is bigger than the other.'

Not a good thing with twins, Emily agreed silently. 'That's why the new doctor is coming to see you. We'll get you settled and sorted before he arrives.'

June glanced at the clock on the wall. 'Is he coming tonight? It's after midnight.'

'Doctors work long hours. And this one is a specialist who's very experienced with twins that are different sized.'

'Oh.' June settled back in the bed and forced herself to breathe calmly through the next contraction.

'I've a tablet here for you that should help the contractions ease off while we wait. It's also used as a blood-pressure tablet so I need to check that before I give it to you.'

Emily wrapped the blood-pressure cuff around June's arm and pumped it up to check. Normal. Good. 'I'll check again in thirty minutes and if you're still having contractions we'll give you another then.'

June was well settled before the sound of

voices drifted to her room. Emily completed her paperwork and put the chart in the tray at the end of the bed. 'Ah. Here's your doctor.' Lily brought Dr D'Arvello into June's room.

Lily winked from behind his shoulder and Emily chewed her lip to keep back the smile.

'Hello, there.' His eyebrows rose when he recognised Emily. He glanced at her badge. 'Sister Cooper?'

'Doctor.' He looked less immaculate than he had earlier today, with a subtle darkness of new growth over his strong chin and his hair unruly across his forehead as if he'd repeatedly pushed it back. Unfortunately he looked even more wickedly attractive.

'Ah.' She saw him file that away before he turned to their patient with a smile that had June relax back into the bed. Nearly as good as calming breaths, Emily thought, with a tinge of sardonic amusement.

'And this is June, who is expecting twins?' He shook June's hand. 'I am Marco D'Arvello. Congratulations.' He pulled the chair across and sat down as if it wasn't really midnight and he hadn't been at work all day.

Like he had all the time in the world to talk to June. Emily liked that. Not what she needed—to find something else she liked about this guy—but she was pleased for June.

June breathed through another contraction, though this one lasted less than twenty seconds. Marco frowned. 'She still threatens labour?'

'That one was shorter after just one dose of the Nifedipine.'

'Good.' He smiled at June. 'Your babies are better off inside at their age so we hope the contractions stop. I've looked at your ultrasounds, June, and your twins have a problem that I think I can help you with.'

June squared her shoulders. 'What sort of problem.'

He smiled. 'I like a woman who gets straight to the point.' Emily tried not to file that away.

'Because your babies share the one placenta, even though they use their own part of the placenta, it seems there's an extra blood vessel connecting their blood supply that shouldn't be there. The problem with that is one twin often gets the lion's share of oxygen and nutrients while the other can be quite disadvantaged.'

'Is it dangerous?' June was nothing if not focussed. Emily felt like hugging the girl.

'For the less fortunate foetus, it certainly can be.'

June turned to look at Emily and then back at Marco. 'You said you can help?'

He nodded. 'I offer you the option of an operation with a small instrument that enters your uterus through the abdomen and seals off the unwanted blood vessel between the twins. We use a tiny laser.'

June's eyes widened with distress? 'A laser? Near my babies? And you've done this before?'

'Dozens of times.' He smiled and Emily felt soothed just watching him. 'Believe me...' he smiled again '...I would do it very carefully but the risks are greater if I do not attempt this closure of the extra vessel.'

He was skilled with reassurance, too, Emily thought, but she could see June's apprehension so she tried to help with the little she knew. 'It sounds like science fiction, doesn't it?'

She gestured to Marco. 'Dr D'Arvello is consulting here on a secondment. Intrauterine surgery is his specialty and he's here to help our obstetric and paediatric surgeons increase their skills.'

June narrowed her gaze. 'So you're the expert?'

'*Si.*' Marco nodded.

'So you don't deliver babies, then?' June frowned. 'Just laser them?'

White teeth flashed as he grinned, and Emily could feel her own mouth curve because he just made her want to smile. 'But no. I am present for many births. Thankfully, only few babies need what I offer and a normal birth is always a joy.' He glanced at Emily. 'You would agree, Sister Cooper?'

'Of course.' Emily wondered if he did see many normal births. Nowadays, at Sydney Harbour Hospital anyway, obstetricians were usually only called when complications occurred. Or for hands-on service for their private patients, but perhaps it was different in Italy.

June had thought it through and now she nodded. 'So what happens now?'

'Tonight we give you the second injection to encourage your twins' lungs to mature in case premature labour cannot be stopped.' He glanced at Emily who inclined her head in agreement. 'And please, no more food or fluids until after we operate tomorrow morning.'

June chewed her lip as the closeness of the operation sank in. 'What time will they come for me?'

'It will be soon after breakfast.' He smiled. 'Which is not for you.'

She pretended to sigh at that and Emily wanted to hug her for being so brave, though the anxiety lay clearly behind her joking manner. 'Thank you, Doctor.'

Marco narrowed his eyes and studied her. 'You have a mother's courage. Would you like something to help you sleep? Sister could give you something to help you relax.'

'No. Thank you. I guess I won't be doing much tomorrow and I can catch up then.'

Marco stood up. '*Bene.* Goodnight, then.' He

caught Emily's eye. 'May I have a word with you, Sister?'

Emily nodded. 'One minute.' And smiled at June. 'I'll be back soon. Would you like a drink of water before I take it away?'

June swallowed half a glass and Emily collected the water and followed him out to the desk, where he was writing up his orders for the night.

CHAPTER TWO

EMILY glanced at the clock. A quarter to one. Dr D'Arvello would have little sleep before his surgery day. She wondered if he was as used to lack of sleep as she was.

From her height above where he sat at the desk she couldn't help noticing the thickness of his dark hair. No sign of grey but he must be in his mid-thirties. A few years older than her and so much more experienced with the world. That deficit hadn't bothered her before. Why should it now? Silly. 'You wished to see me, Doctor?'

His dark eyes swept up from the notes and over her face. He smiled and she found herself grinning back like a goose before she could stop herself. 'I did not know you were a midwife at your daughter's visit this morning.'

It felt so long ago. 'It's not important?'

He frowned. 'But I would have offered more explanation if you wished. Is there more I can tell you?'

'No. Thank you.' She shrugged, a little embarrassed to admit it. 'Of course I have researched the internet and read what I can find. I think I understand the operation well enough.'

He nodded. 'Sometimes I wish my clients would not look up on the internet but I am sure you picked well with your sites. The procedure is fairly simple. Perhaps a little more complicated than June's surgery, but over almost as quickly.'

He stood up, towered over her again, and seemed to hesitate. 'And will you have to come to work tomorrow night after your daughter's operation?'

Her stomach dropped with a tinge of alarm.

Was there bad news he hadn't mentioned? 'Actually, I'm not.' Did he think she would be too upset?

Still he frowned. 'So when will you sleep?'

'I'll go home as soon as Annie is out of surgery. So I will sleep when she does, afterwards.'

'You will be tired.' He handed her the completed notes and she took them and stared at the pages. Not really seeing his looping scrawl. Looked anywhere but his face. It had been a while since anyone had wondered if she was tired and his kindness made her feel strange. This whole conversation was surreal because she was so ridiculously conscious of him.

She risked a glance. 'I was just thinking the same for you.'

He shrugged his manly shoulders and she felt her stomach kick. This was crazy. She was way too aware of this man, this transient doctor. 'I sleep less than four hours a night. Always have done.'

'And I survive on about the same. I'm used to it.' She opened the folder at the medication page. She needed to get this injection for June happening. The last one had been given twelve hours ago at the regional hospital. 'So we have something in common.'

He wasn't ready to let her go. 'Perhaps we have more than that.'

She blinked. 'I don't know what you mean?'

He smiled but there was mischief that made her cheeks pink again. 'A concern and empathy for our patients.'

What had she thought he meant? 'Oh. Of course. Well, thank you for your concern. I'll just go for the hydrocortisone for June.'

'Perhaps one more thing?' He held up one finger. 'The reason I asked.'

She stopped. 'I'm sorry?'

'Tomorrow night. Because your daughter will be in the hospital. Perhaps you will need diversion from worry. It is Friday.'

She didn't get it. 'And?'

'A favour. I have promised myself a dinner on your so beautiful Sydney Harbour. I am only here for a month. It would be more pleasant to have company.'

Good grief. He was asking her out. On a date? 'I'm sure lots of ladies would love to be your company.'

He shrugged, as if aware what she said was true, not with conceit but with disinterest. 'I would prefer you.'

Normally he had no problem asking a beautiful woman to dinner. So why was this difficult? He just wanted to enjoy a diversion with this woman, not ask her to have his babies. Why stumble around like a callow youth when she obviously wanted to get on with her work?

It seemed his offer was the last thing she'd expected. He did not think shock was a good reaction and waited with unusual tension while she recovered.

'Well, I guess you won't run away because you find I have a teenage daughter.'

'This has happened?'

'Imagine.' She turned away. 'Anyway. Thank you. But, no, thank you. I don't date.'

'But this is not a date. Just kindness on your part.'

She raised her eyebrows. 'Really? Tricky. Then perhaps I could let you know tomorrow. In the mean time, you could keep looking. Now I must get back to June.'

'*Bene.* Of course. *Buonanotte.*'

'Goodnight.'

Marco left the ward with a smile on his face. It had seemed fortuitous to find the woman who had whispered through his brain at odd moments all day, unexpectedly, on this maternity ward.

A midwife, no less, and someone he would see a little of in the course of his work. And he had planned to dine on the harbour at some stage, though perhaps not tomorrow. And she intrigued him—though a conquest might not be easy. Always a challenge he could not resist.

But with sudden clarity he'd realised that Emily would be unlikely to leave her daughter unattended, except for work, when they lived together. So it had to be tomorrow or the next night or not at all. He smiled to himself. Perhaps her doctor could keep Annie in an extra night for rest. Bad doctor.

He didn't know why he was so sure there was no man in Emily's life, but she had the look of an untouched woman, and he trusted his instincts. She said she did not date. At least that instinct had been correct. A date would be good for her.

She hadn't said yes but that made it all more interesting. The degree of anticipation he could feel building already made him smile. He'd brushed off the need for appreciation and commitment, had had it leached out of him throughout his dark childhood, but a harmless dalliance could hurt no one and he would give much for Emily Cooper to look on his invitation with approval. But not until tomorrow would he find out.

Emily's night passed quickly and thankfully without time for the distraction of Marco D'Arvello's unexpected invitation. June's premature contractions settled, but the arrival of two women in labour, one after the other, left little time for her to work out how she was going to turn him down.

When Emily finished her shift the sun shone through the windshield straight into her eyes as she drove home to the little cottage above the pier at Balmain East she'd inherited from her gran.

On night duty public transport didn't work. Through the days she caught ferries. She couldn't actually see Sydney harbour from her windows but the swish of the wash on the shore from passing boats floated in her window at night as she dressed for work.

Annie was pacing the front veranda as she waited for her mother to arrive home.

'Why did you have to be late, today of all days?'

Emily carried her bag into the house and tried not to sigh. 'We've been busy. I didn't dawdle for the fun of it.'

Annie dropped her complaints and hugged her mother warmly. 'Sorry. I'm nervous…' she twisted her fingers '…and started to worry we'd be late.' She shook her head. 'And baby was awake and moving most of the night. It's almost as if she's nervous too.'

'I wouldn't be surprised if she was. Babies pick up on their mother's mood.'

Annie tilted her head and studied her mother. 'Well, I can see you need a cup of tea so maybe I can pick up yours too. I made you raisin toast!' It was a large statement. In case Emily didn't get the significance she added, 'Even though I'm starving myself because I have to fast.'

Emily was pleased to see after the initial stress Annie had calmed down. And was being nice. Though the last thing she wanted to do was eat. Her stomach was in knots about Annie's hospital visit and impending anaesthetic for both her and her tiny granddaughter. 'Thank you for that. Saves me a few minutes while I shower and dress.'

Three hours later Emily put down the crossword. The surgery seemed to be taking for ever.

The waiting-room magazines needed to be tossed into the bin and replaced. Still, Emily had flicked through them all. She'd chewed her nails down to the quick. Now she was onto the edge of her finger. Come on!

At ten-thirty the theatre doors swung open and Marco D'Arvello strode through them. It seemed his focussed glance searched until he found her sitting along the wall.

She bolted upright off her chair as if on a spring. In seconds he was at her side. 'It is good. All went well.'

Emily sagged. Thank God. A strange buzzing began in her ears and her face felt funny, numb. The room began to tilt. His arms came up to steady her shoulders and he steered her back into a sitting position. His head dipped towards her with concern. 'Sit. Not so fast. Have you eaten?'

'What?' The room stopped its slow turn and

the humming noises in her ears faded away. She closed and opened her eyes slowly.

'Emily? Have you eaten?'

His hands left her shoulders and she felt strangely bereft, almost tempted to catch them back. 'Must have got up too fast.'

'*Si.*'

Had she eaten? She couldn't remember. 'Um. Raisin toast three hours ago.'

'Come. We will go for a cocoa and some more of your raisin toast before you drive home and go to bed. Annie is not yet awake but will be back in the ward in about thirty minutes. I will return with you then to see her.'

Now she felt silly. Imagine if she'd fainted at his feet. 'I'm fine. Just stood too fast. I'm sure you have better things to do than drink cocoa with me.'

'I cannot think of one.' He shrugged with that Latin assurance Italian men seemed to have and her brain couldn't function enough to think of a good excuse to decline. She had to admit the thought of not being alone for another thirty minutes was attractive.

He went on. 'I believe the prognosis for both your Annie and our friend June's babies has improved significantly. I can do no more for the moment.' He searched her face and seemed satisfied. 'Your colour has improved. But another half an hour of waiting without food will not help.' He held out his hand. 'Come.'

Bossy man. Though she was feeling better. 'You say that a lot.'

He looked puzzled. 'What is that?'

She dropped her chin and deepened her voice in imitation. 'Come!'

He inclined his head. 'I will attempt to refrain.'

They smiled at each other. Such quaint speech patterns and it seemed he could cope with teasing. Luckily. What had got into her? She picked up her bag and glanced at her watch.

'Then thank you. A hot drink would be nice. I start to get cold when I need to sleep. Just twenty minutes and I'll come back.'

'*Si.* Your daughter should be back in the ward soon after that.'

They turned a few heads when they walked into the tea shop in the hospital grounds. Or Marco did, Emily thought as necks swivelled. She didn't actually know many of the staff, having worked in Maternity on nights most of her career, and not a frequent visitor to the kiosk either, but she'd bet someone would recognise them and spread the word.

This place was a minefield of gossip. Another reason she preferred nights.

There was Head of Surgery Finn Kennedy and Evie Lockheart, her friend she was to have coffee with later in the week with Lily. Evie was hospital royalty and heiress to the Lockheart fortune.

Evie and Finn sat, head to head, engrossed in a deep and meaningful conversation, and to her surprise Evie slid her hand across the table and gripped Finn's hand. Emily couldn't help wondering if something terrible had happened.

Evie's father had been kind to her all those years ago when she'd been a sixteen-year-old mother of an ill prem baby, and he'd been the one who'd suggested she would make a great nurse. He'd even provided the reference needed to start work as an unskilled nurse assistant until she could manage the extra burden of study. She liked Evie.

Finn, she was just happy to stay out of his way. He was a grouch. The hospital's most experienced surgeon, though rumours had begun to circulate that he suffered some kind of medical problem that was threatening his career.

Emily had enough on her plate. She didn't want to get anywhere near more drama and she steered Marco to the furthest corner of the kiosk.

More heads swivelled their way and instead of ducking her head she lifted her chin and smiled and nodded back.

Maybe she was sick of being boring. Ungossip-worthy. Now she was the mother of a pregnant teenager, cavorting with the new Italian O and G consultant, and flaunting it all in the daylight hours, she may as well hold her head up.

Something had changed her. Marco sensed the stiffening of her shoulders and resisted the sudden urge to take her elbow. Surely she was used to people admiring her? Even bruised around the eyes from lack of sleep, she was a stunning woman.

He'd thought her attractive yesterday, but seeing her this morning when he'd left Theatre, she'd reminded him of a fragile Madonna and a strange urge to protect her had welled uncomfortably in his throat. A sudden desire to cradle her worried face in his hands and reassure her.

No doubt she would have something to say about him trying that and he shook off the uneasiness that feeling left him with. She stopped at a table that couldn't be described as secluded but it seemed it would do. Marco pulled out her chair.

'You are smiling? Something amuses you?'

'Gossip.'

He glanced around. 'In a hospital as large as this?'

'Especially in this hospital.' She followed his gaze. Tried not to look at Evie and Finn. 'I hate gossip. It lives and breathes other people's business. And here I am with the handsome Italian doctor who has operated on my daughter. I'm never seen with anyone.'

'At least you notice something about me.'

'You're a bit hard to miss.'

He looked around. 'I too despise gossip.' The memories tasted bitter in his mouth.

Emily heard the underlying resentment and wondered where that had come from. The waitress arrived as soon as they'd picked up the menu and Emily put it down again and smiled at the girl. 'We've only twenty minutes. Should we order food?'

'Sure. Promise I'll be quick. What would you like?'

She looked at Marco. 'Scones and cream?'

Marco smiled at the young girl and she blushed all the way to the roots of her hair. 'One hot chocolate, one coffee black, and two scones and cream. *Per favore.*' The girl nodded and sped off.

Well, that was that. She studied his face. He didn't look tired. So maybe he really did manage on four hours' sleep. She was beginning to droop. She stifled a yawn. 'So tell me how it went.'

'Very well. No complications. A simple scope and shunt away from the narrowed opening into the bladder. Initial ultrasound shows good drainage into the bladder already.'

'Do you think my granddaughter's kidneys will be very damaged?'

His face softened and he reached across to touch her hand. Just that one stroke made her feel better. Comforted. His hand moved back. 'This I cannot tell. We will hope not.'

What did she expect? How could he know that? She just wanted reassurance but wisely he had promised nothing he couldn't give. Still, she appreciated his empathy. He was a kind man.

The hot drinks and scones arrived and they both smiled at the waitress. 'So quick. *Grazie.*'

'Wow.' Emily too was impressed. 'Thank you.' The girl grinned and hurried off and almost bumped into Finn, who stood suddenly from his chair, almost knocking it over.

He growled something at their waitress and shook off Evie's hand before he stormed towards the door. Evie's face looked white and drawn and Emily looked away. Maybe she could catch up with Evie later. Check she was okay. There was no doubt she was in love with the man who had just left her and Emily felt her heart go out to the younger woman. She'd picked a hard road there.

'It seems our surgical chief is not happy.' Marco too had seen.

She refocussed on the man beside her. 'I'm sorry?'

'Finn. We met in the States a few years ago. Got on well.'

Of course Marco would know him. They were both surgeons. She spread cream on the scone and then dropped a dollop of jam in the middle.

'Evie's tough. If anyone can bounce back from Finn's ill humour, Evie can.'

'And who is she?'

'A medical officer here, a darned good one, but she's more than that. Her father's the hospital's main benefactor, and the reason Sydney Harbour has so many ground-breaking programs.'

'Lockheart?'

'Yes. If rumour is to be believed, she and Finn have an on-again, off-again relationship that sometimes rattles the windows around here. But if I needed medical help, either of them would do fine by me.'

And you would do fine by me, he thought, and the premonition that this woman could rock his stable skim-the-surface world seeped into his bones with a wary premonition. 'I realise you have a lot on your mind but have you thought about dinner this evening?'

'No.' Not much anyway. 'I really can't think of anything until after I see Annie.'

'Of course. Forgive me.' He was not usually this impatient.

They sipped their drinks and the silence became a little strained. She broke it. 'So how long are you here? At Sydney Harbour?'

'A month. Then I fly out to the US for a consultancy in New York. Last month it was London.'

She sipped her cocoa and the heat seeped into her cold edges. His life sounded a little on the cool side too.

Suddenly she wasn't hungry. 'It sounds a glamorous life.' The creamy scone stared back at her. Like a red eye. She bet she had red eyes. Why on earth had this man asked her to breakfast? Kindness. That was all. Now she just needed to accept the favour and move on.

'*Si*. Glamorous.' He picked up his coffee and took a sip.

'So where is home?' At his frown she tried again. 'Your family.'

His expression didn't change but she felt stillness come over him. And the temperature dropped another two degrees. So he didn't like questions. 'I have no family. I rent when I need. Mostly I work.'

'I'm sorry. I didn't mean to pry.' She glanced at her watch and took another sip of her cocoa. 'I might see if Annie is back.'

He'd been abrupt. Closed her out like he always did when people asked about his family. No wonder she wanted to leave. What did he expect to happen? He never answered questions about himself. He'd learnt at a very young age when the police were eager for any news of his father. When neighbours had shunned his family as soon as they'd realised who they were.

But this woman would never do that. The voice came from nowhere. Just a whisper, like she'd whispered yesterday to his thoughts, and he closed his ears.

'I apologise.' He glanced down at her uneaten scone. 'Your food.'

'I'm not really hungry.' She yawned. 'Excuse me.' He wanted to pick her up and carry her to a big feather bed and tuck her in to sleep. Or not to sleep.

He glanced around for the waitress and managed to catch her eye. She nodded and started their way.

'We will go. See if Annie is back on the ward and then you must go home to bed.' There was that thought again. Emily in bed. He dragged his mind away from her golden bob of hair lying next to his on the pillow.

She dug into her bag for her wallet and he shook his head. 'Please. Allow me.' He laid a note on the table and stood up to help pull out her chair. The waitress arrived and he smiled and gestured with his hand that she keep the change.

Emily stood and he followed her out of the kiosk back towards the wards. He wanted to ask if she would come with him tonight but he would not ask again. Perhaps after she'd seen her daughter he would know.

CHAPTER THREE

'HI, MA,' Annie whispered sleepily. 'They said my baby's fine.' She lay in a twin-bed room and the other stood turned back, waiting for June to return to the ward. 'I'm gonna call her Rosebud.'

Emily ached with the thick swell of love in her throat. At the moment her daughter could call her daughter Medusa and she wouldn't mind. She was just glad Annie and her baby were okay. It was hard to realise her own baby was growing up. She didn't want to think about the time when she left her completely. And her little gnome granddaughter was safe from further harm too. 'That's wonderful, darling.' She squeezed the pale fingers on the sheet and stared mistily down at her daughter.

'It all went very well, Annie.' Marco's deep voice rumbled in her ear and his presence felt like a man they'd known a lot longer than twenty-four hours.

Emily stepped back to think about that, but he must have stepped forward at the same time.

His hands came up to rest on her shoulders and her shoulders fitted snugly up against a wall of chest she'd only dreamed about. It felt too good to move but Emily's attention flew to her daughter. Thankfully Annie's long lashes rested on her pale cheeks as she drifted in a post-anaesthetic haze and she couldn't see her mother's weakness.

From the pillow Annie's eyelids didn't flicker as her voice faded away. 'Thank you, Marco.' In her semi-doze Annie's palm slid across the sheet to protect the small mound of her stomach and Emily let herself relax for a moment.

Just enjoy the sensation of being held.

Take the comfort he was no doubt offering. She hadn't had a lot of that lately. Especially since Gran had died.

But this was different from Gran's gentle love. This was a virulent, protector of a man saying he was there for her, if only for the duration of her daughter's recovery, and she'd be a fool to not accept it for what it was. She didn't want to think about how some women had this twenty-four seven. It felt too damn good.

But it wasn't reality. She stepped away. 'I'll visit this afternoon, darling.'

Annie opened her eyes. 'Um. No. Don't. I'm just gonna sleep. See me tomorrow, Mum. Have a rest.'

Emily winced. 'If that's what you want.' She chewed her lip. 'You sure? I'll have my phone. Just leave a message on my phone and I'll come in.'

Annie nodded sleepily. 'Tomorrow. Love you.'

'Love you, baby.' She hesitated. Watched her daughter sink into a heavier sleep.

Marco steered her towards the door. 'Come.'

She flicked a glance at him and he grinned. 'I do not know another word. Leave does not seem to work the same.'

She smiled back. 'Come is fine.'

'Then—' he deepened his voice to a tease '—come.' They grinned at each other. 'She looks well, your Annie, and we can hope not too much damage is done. But for now, sleepyhead, are you going to go home to worry?'

'No. I don't think I will.' She'd try not to and think about leaning back into Marco's arms. 'I think I'll sleep well.'

'Good.'

Then she thought of tonight, of the empty house. Of waking this afternoon after the four hours' sleep she never seemed to be able to improve on, and wondering what it would have been like to go out with this handsome man, do something that would take her mind off the worry. Or she could sit at home and think about Annie. And maybe one day she could go on a dinner cruise on Sydney harbour on her own.

'I'm wondering...' She hesitated but he'd stopped and his attention was fully on her. 'Um. Dinner. What time?'

She had to guess he hadn't found anyone between hot chocolate and now.

So that was how she came to be dressed, waiting, scanning herself in the mirror. Wondering if the top was too old, should she wear a scarf? Could she still walk in high heels—it had been so long!

The doorbell drilled her like a cold knife and she glared at the mirror. Nerves. She was a big girl, dump the nerves, put on the smile and let the man take you out. You know you fancy him and he's only here for a month.

This would be good practice for the time when Annie left for her own life. He'd said he'd pick her up so he had a car, must have hired one if he was only here for a month. She kept coming back to that. Just a month. Too short to lose her heart. She hoped.

She peeked out from behind the lace curtain. She hadn't expected an Aston Martin. Or the open-necked black shirt. He was standing at the door. Looking around. Waiting for her to answer, and she was watching him with nerves flapping like pelicans in her belly.

Marco breathed in. Was unexpectedly aware of the late afternoon light, as if he should remember this moment. The slosh of waves and chug of boats on the harbour a few houses away. The tang of salt and seaweed.

The drift of voices from homes close to Emily's. People who saw this woman every day. Probably had for years. How could she still be alone? How had some man not scooped her up and carried her and her daughter off?

When would she answer this door? He checked the number again just as the door opened.

His breath was expelled in a sigh. A woman with such style. *'Bellisima.'* Every time he saw her she captured more of his attention. Appeared more exquisite.

'Thank you. Come through.' She gestured to the quaint sitting area with the carved wooden archway between the rooms.

Emily smoothed her coral skirt, willing the heat in her cheeks to subside as she invited him in. He looked pretty hot himself in immaculate black trousers and a silk shirt that screamed Italian tailor.

If he only knew. She didn't spend money on

clothes. Only the occasional piece of underwear she still felt guilty about and hid from her daughter. Gran's skirt and antique lace blouse, even her lovely silver dancing shoes were sixty years old but fitted perfectly. She'd always been Gran's size since she'd had Annie.

Sixteen years the same size. Except for the last few months when the one loving person in her life had faded away to a wisp of her former self.

'The boat leaves at six. Forgive me if I rush you but it is to catch the sunset on the water.'

Not the time for sad memories.

Tonight she would embrace life and a handsome man.

She'd forgotten how good it felt to dress up and see her escort light up when he saw her. See his eyes smoulder, sweep over her, want her. Not that she was thinking that. But sixteen years was too long between attempted seductions so it would be nice to see if she still had feminine wiles.

He was waiting. 'I'll just get my purse.' She leant past him to the hall table and picked up her filmy wrap as well as her tiny clutch. 'A night on the harbour is worth the rush.'

He stepped forward and took the wrap from her hands. 'Allow me,'he said, and spread the floating silk over her shoulders. She tried not to shiver with the sensation. 'My car is downstairs.' She focussed on transport—much safer.

'Is it worth having a car when you work such long hours?' She was still gabbling as she pulled the door shut after him.

'*Si.*' He waited for her to precede him down the steps and she could feel his presence solid behind her. It felt strange, to say the least. She felt strange. Like a teen. She really did need to get out more.

'I have rented an apartment across the bay near the clown's face and I am often called in.'

'Of course.' Not tonight, she hoped.

'Not tonight, though.'

She smiled as he answered her thought and glanced towards the harbour. Imagining the bright mouth of the amusement-park entrance. 'So you're near Luna Park. Do you look down on it? Can you hear the children screaming on the rides?'

Gran used to take her and Annie. For a few years it had been sadly neglected but she'd heard it had been renovated and new life breathed into the attractions.

'A little. It makes me smile. But my windows face mainly across the harbour and the bridge. The view is as good as anywhere I have travelled.'

'You could have caught the ferry from Milson's Point to me here. Just get off at Balmain East.'

'*Si*. Perhaps another day. But tonight I prefer the privacy of my own vehicle.'

He unlocked the car and waited for her to sit with her skirt straightened before he closed the door. Within seconds he was slipping in beside her and suddenly the car shrank to a tiny womb of warm air imbued with a faint tang of his aftershave.

She was really here. In a car with a gorgeous Italian man intent on sharing the evening with her. He'd said he only wanted her company. She couldn't remember the last time she'd been out with a man and felt like this.

Gran and her knitting buddies had nudged her into a movie or two with men she'd met but each time they'd withdrawn when they'd realised how much time she needed to spend with Annie.

He gestured to the houses and trees around her home. 'You must love living here.'

'Yep. I walk around the bay to catch a ferry

to the city on my days off. Or just walk around the harbour.'

He leaned forward and started the engine. 'Your harbour is incredible but I probably see more of it from the hospital windows.' He shrugged those lovely shoulders of his and she tried not to stare. 'Except at night before sleep.'

She didn't want to think of Marco sleeping, or maybe she did, because the picture came anyway. Black boxers? Or those hipster undies the male models wore that clung. Also in black. No shirt. Silk sheets. Stretched out across the mattress. Whoa.

What on earth had they been talking about before her mind had gone AWOL? View watching? 'Perhaps you should do less work hours.'

He grinned at her. All white teeth and vibrant male who scorned the thought of taking things easy. 'For what reason? I like to give my job everything.'

'Um. Life just might speed by.'

He glanced at her as they waited to turn onto a busy road. 'Has life sped by for you, Emily?'

'I'm thinking the last sixteen years have.' She loved the way he drawled her name. Emerrrleee.

The way it rolled from his lips with that sexy undertone. She'd never really felt she'd arrived in the sexy department but, hey, there was a first for everything, and Gran's blouse was firm across her breasts. Must be why she was so conscious of her curves tonight.

Conversation remained desultory until they arrived. She'd expected a shiny white mini cruise ship like she saw most times ablaze with lights and four decks high with tuxedoed waiters. Five star, sit behind glass, no nasty breeze to muck up your hair. She didn't get that.

What she got was a hundred-year-old tall ship, three masted and dark polished wood. He ushered her up the wooden gangway on the side of the ship and they were met by a very official-looking captain with a feathered hat.

His staff was dressed in period costume, sailors and maidservants from a bygone era, the few tables grouped in secluded areas of the deck set with lace and crystal and the dull glint of genuine silverware.

Marco watched her. Enjoyed her reaction. Her eyes widened with wonder and she turned to look up at him. 'Wow...' The word was soft but his heart warmed at the genuine delight he could see in her face.

'How did you find out about this? I thought they were only privately hired.'

'Your Dr Finn. He's been very helpful.'

Finn helpful? He must have read her face because he smiled and said, 'He is a man's man, perhaps.'

She thought of Evie. Or a strong woman's man.

Grumpy Finn even knowing about something like this was hard to take in but she didn't care.

She much preferred a man who had gentleness and a way that made her feel at ease. Though a little sexual attraction wasn't going astray. Like Marco? What was wrong with her tonight? She needed to remember where fact lay and fantastic fiction fell. She rested her hand on his arm. 'This is great. I love it. Thank you.'

His hand came up to cover hers. 'And I am glad.' The captain gestured to their table and helped her sit.

The best seats. They were seated at the stern and she could glance behind her to the water slapping gently against the hull. The masts soared into the sky in front of her.

They hadn't made it with much time to spare. The rattle of the wooden gangplank echoed across the water as it was pulled in. The scurry of sailors as mooring ropes were untied and the boat drifted quietly away from the wharf. She glanced up with amazement as figures overhead leant on cross spars to pull ropes and loosen the smaller topsails.

'This is incredible.' Suddenly she was aware she hadn't eaten since her nibble at the scones that morning.

'Yes,' he said, but he was watching her face. A tiny smile on his lips as her gaze darted about, each new sight making her eyes widen and her mouth open.

Champagne appeared on a tray and he took two glasses and offered her one. Absently she smiled and sipped and he could barely contain his amusement to see her so involved in the business of preparing the ship.

'You really love this.'

Her eyes were shining. 'Yes.'

He'd thought he had his walls up, solid, impenetrable walls around his heart, around his desire to even acknowledge his heart. He was doing all right on his own, had been on his own since he'd left home not long after his mother had died, but watching Emily, savouring her pleasure, this was different. Different from anything he'd felt before. And it was not possible. *Non e'possibile.*

'Aren't you?'

He'd lost the train of conversation. *'Scusi?'*

'Aren't you enjoying this too?' She tilted her head and her cap of golden hair swung across her cheek. His fingers itched to reach out and brush it back from her face. It looked like silk. It would feel like silk. Such a caring face for one so beautiful.

This was outside his experience. Usually the more beautiful the woman the more shallow the water. Emily was not such a person. She waited for his answer with anticipation clear in her eyes.

'*Si*, the night is very special. You are very special.'

She blushed again and glanced out over the water. 'I wasn't fishing.'

'Of course not.' This he did not understand. 'You have no rod.' He glanced around. 'You wish to fish?'

She laughed. A throaty, infectious giggle she tried to hide behind her hand. Now, why would she try to hide such a thing of joy?

The waiter came. 'Evenin', all.' Dressed like an English officer, he took their orders and re-filled their glasses. Emily grinned at him and the waiter grinned back. Marco frowned.

She looked back at him. 'I mean I wasn't look-ing for a compliment. I don't want to catch a fish.' She laughed again and he had to smile back at her.

Her face glowed. Like the first time he'd seen her. 'I see. A colloquialism. You Australians have many of them. Like the English.'

'My gran married an Englishman. She told me

he always said "give me a butcher's hook" instead of "give me a look". It was funny when she said it.' She smiled at the memory. He'd never seen a woman smile so much. It warmed his cold soul.

'Tell me about your family. Your parents. Your gran.'

She put her glass down and rested her chin in her hands. 'My parents? They're both dead. But they were very strict, traditional, not at all suited to having an unwed pregnant teenager for a daughter.'

He nodded. 'I see.' She could tell he did.

'My gran? She loved me unconditionally. Like I love my daughter. One day I hope to find a relationship like that.'

From a man who could lay down roots and be there for her. One who didn't immerse himself in his work for a limited time and then pack bags and leave without looking back. Not like him. 'But not the father of your Annie?'

She shrugged. 'His family were wealthy. Too good for me. Once the scandal broke he was packed off. We never saw him again.'

He could not comprehend this. 'Never?' Then no doubt she was too good for him. *Bastardo.* 'He has never seen his daughter?'

'Never.' She broke her bread roll, picked up her knife and stabbed the butter. He flinched. She looked up and grinned at his expression.

'I got over his lack of interest years ago. Though for Annie's sake I'd have liked him to have made some contact. His parents send money every year on her birthday and I put it in trust. When she's twenty-one she can do what she likes with it.'

She spread her butter and took a bite with her tiny white teeth just as the entrée arrived. He thought with amusement it was good she'd put the knife down or the sailor could have been frightened.

'Ooh. Calamari. I love calamari. What's the Italian word for calamari?' She made short work of her few pieces and he held back his smile. He liked a woman who didn't play with her food.

'I'm sorry.' He grinned. 'The same. Calamari.' He glanced down at his tiny fillets of fish on the bed of lettuce. 'But the word for fish is *pesce.*'

'*Pesce*,' she repeated. 'It almost sounds like fishee.' She grinned and watched him put the last one in his mouth and he was very conscious of the direction of her eyes. 'Your English is very good. Much better than my Italian.'

He swallowed the delicious fillet in his mouth without tasting it, his appetite elsewhere. 'I have spent a lot of time out of Italy.' He changed the subject back to her. 'So you went into nursing after your Annie was born?'

She patted her coral lips with her napkin and

his attention, again, was caught. It took him a moment to catch up when she spoke. 'Annie was in Neonatal Intensive Care. She was four weeks early. A prem that took a long time to feed.'

She glanced up at him. 'I never missed a feed in the three weeks she was there and I fell in love with the midwives. With the special-care nursery. With tiny babies. I'd found what I wanted to do. And Gran, not my parents, supported me.'

He could see her. A vigilant young teen mum with her tiny baby. Turning up, night and day, to be there for her daughter. Incredible. The more he found out, the more she intrigued him.

'Enough about me.' So Emily didn't want to think of the early years. Perhaps what she'd missed out on in her younger days.

She glanced around the ship. 'They must have engines as well because I don't think they have enough sail on to make it move this fast. Can we walk around? Check out the other side of the ship?' She glanced towards the thick mast. 'Touch things?'

She could touch him. 'You wish to touch something?' She picked up on his double meaning and flicked him a warning glance. He was glad the knife was on her plate. She amused him.

'*Si*. Of course.' He stood and helped pull out her chair. Then he crooked his arm and to his delight she slid her hand through and he savoured the feel of her fingers against his skin.

They strolled the deck and the magic of the night fell over them like the soft wrap she wore around her shoulders.

The lights of the harbour twinkled and shone across the water, ferries and paddle-wheel dinner cruisers floated past, and occasionally the sound of a band floated across from a party barge filled with revellers.

This was so much better, to have Emily quietly beside him. Few couples were walking, and the awareness between them grew with the unexpected privacy a bulkhead or a thick mast could provide.

Always the Sydney Harbour Bridge dominated the skyline, they passed under it, the soaring iron structure a thing of great beauty lit like a golden arch, and it receded and became even more magical with distance.

He wished he could hold onto this moment so that he could pack it away in his suitcase when he left here. Perhaps to remove and examine one lonely night in a hotel room on the other side of the world. *Stupido.*

This would all be over too quickly.

CHAPTER FOUR

Two hours later Emily held his hand as they stepped off the gangplank of the tall ship and sighed as she stepped back onto terra firma. 'A wonderful dinner. Thank you.'

'The night does not have to be over yet.' He squeezed her fingers.

They watched a ferry come in and there was something vibrant about the noisy reverse of the engines that churned up the water and the delayed slap of heavier waves on the pier as the deckhand jumped off and secured the vessel to a wharfside cleat.

'That's my ferry,' Emily pointed. 'It docks two minutes from my door and goes on to Luna Park jetty. You could have taken the ferry and walked up the hill to your apartment.'

He glanced across the water as other ferries did their business. 'Would you like to take it now? I can return for my car tomorrow. It is safe. We could have more time on the water. Perhaps stroll around your Luna Park, eat an ice cream?'

'Or fairy floss?'

He squeezed her hand. 'Fairy floss?'

'Pink balls of spun sugar. A dreadfully evil sweet.'

A wicked look. 'Dreadfully evil is good.'

It would be silly to leave his car in the car park. Mad to jump on a ferry just because of a whim and walk around an amusement park at nine at night. She so wanted to do that.

She gave in to the child within. 'Let's.'

So they did. She explained how the vending machines spat out the ferry tickets, dragged him up to the front of the boat so they could get blown to pieces on the deserted bow, and they lifted their faces to the spray. 'This is much faster than our sailing boat.'

She looked back at their beautiful three-masted vessel. 'Not quite as romantic.'

His arm slipped around her shoulders and he turned her to face him. 'We could change that?'

She stood on tiptoe as he bent. Met his smiling mouth with hers with a light-hearted press of lips that never intended to be anything else— except for that second farewell light press that deepened just a touch and invited a third quick kiss, which deepened just a little more...

What magic was this? What spell had she cast? Lust slammed into him like their ferry had hit a solid wave and it was Marco who stepped back. If he didn't stop he'd have crushed Emily into him and who knew what might have happened?

Always he had control, was the master of his own desires, but this Emily's sweet innocence gripped him with more power than the most experienced woman and forced him to pull back while he still could.

He wrapped her in his arms and stared over her head at the lights on the edge of the harbour. What was he doing?

He would leave in three weeks. Began to realise she might not know the rules by which he played and did not need the complication he offered. A darker voice within disagreed. Perhaps she did?

Emily snuggled into the warmth of solid muscle. Lo-o-ovely kisses. Mmmmmm. Shame he'd stopped but that was good. She needed to be sensible. She could remember her mother's cold voice very clearly even after all these years. 'Your father and I don't deserve this shame. You're a tramp!' Though how one fumbled night and a broken condom made her a tramp she didn't know. And Gran had shooshed her and said it wasn't true.

Well, she hadn't tramped at all for the last sixteen years. A few pathetic-in-hindsight kisses and a meal or two. No wonder she hadn't been tempted to chase those men. They didn't kiss like this. She felt Marco's arms loosen from the after hug and she guessed it was time to step away.

His hands slid down her shoulders with a lingering reluctance and dropped right away, and she pushed the hair from her eyes so she could see his face. He looked serious. Too serious.

'Is everything okay?' Crikey. Maybe she'd been a hopeless kisser and he was embarrassed.

'You kiss like an angel.'

Her cheeks flamed. Had she said that out loud? He went on with a twisted smile. 'And it seemed prudent to stop.'

Not quite sure how to take that but maybe with

sincere gratitude because it wasn't unreasonable to think that kiss could have led to an embarrassing incident. 'Oh. Well.' She brushed the hair out of her eyes again. 'You're pretty good yourself.'

The ferry pulled into Balmain East, tied up then untied and chugged across the harbour to McMahon's Point. They both watched the busy deckhand with an intensity born of diversion from what they wanted to really do. Marco squeezed her hand and she squeezed back.

When the ferry pulled into Milson's Point wharf, at least they had a purpose as they stepped across the walkway to the pier.

The laughing-clown mouth of the entrance invited them to join the milling crowd and Marco couldn't help looking up at the squealing victims spinning above their heads on a swirling circular ride. His stomach contracted at the thought.

'You like these rides?'

Emily laughed. 'Not those ones. Though I am

partial to the view from the Ferris wheel and a trip on the Wild Mouse.'

'A wild mouse?'

She pointed. 'Up there. It's a mini roller-coaster that makes you think you're going to fly out over the harbour and instead turns the corner suddenly. It's Annie's favourite.'

'It sounds like your favourite. Not Annie's.' This one didn't look too bad. At least it didn't turn upside down.

He crossed to the payment window and purchased a wrist-banded ride pass for both of them.

'Come.' He lingered over the word until she grinned. 'We will see who is the most frightened.'

They jogged up the gaily painted steps hand in hand and Emily turned to him. 'Can't you feel the infectious enthusiasm from the young crowd?'

He wasn't sure if he was infected yet. The

teens were having a ball on this Friday night and her smiling face turned from side to side as she caught glimpses of the screaming occupants… and perhaps seeping some foolishness into him.

A battered little red car on rails trundled across and stopped in front of them with a clang. 'Jump in,' the laconic ride attendant drawled, 'man at the back, lady between his legs. I do the seat belt.' Marco could tell he'd said the same a million times.

This idea improved with time, Marco thought with satisfaction, as Emily snuggled into the space between his legs with her skirt smoothed out in front of her. Nice. Warm and soft and in need of protection during this coming adventure. It was a very small car.

She had to lean back into his chest and his arms came along the outside of hers to grip the same handle. Snug. The car shunted off with an unexpected jerk and Emily was forced back into his chest with a bump. He tightened his hands and prepared to enjoy the ride.

They rolled down the first hill and jolted onto a runner to be pulled up the next and then gathered speed. It blurred after that.

The first sharp corner loomed as they rocketed towards it and he read the sign just before they turned.

'Brace Yourself!'

He braced and Emily slammed into him and he slammed into the side of the car, she laughed and he had to laugh as the next corner came up and it seemed they would sail out over the harbour, but the trusty wheels remained hooked to the track as they flew around that one.

Emily laughed again and he could feel the spread of a huge smile across his face as the ride rocketed on. Up and down steep little hills that lifted them out of their seats as they bounced at the bottom, still stuck together, and he decided then they would repeat this experience before they went home.

The car rolled to a stop. It was over. Shame, that.

'Lady out first. Then the gent. Keep to the left and down the stairs.'

Emily waited for him to climb out, not as elegantly as he could have wished but that smile seemed glued to his face and she laughed at his expression. 'You'd think you'd never been to an amusement park before.'

The laughter fell away. No.

He tried not to think of his lonely childhood, his family moving towns in the dead of night, and those periods of abject poverty when his father had been in gaol.

'Oh!' She was not slow. The smile she threw him would have lit the whole harbour in a power failure. 'In that case, we need to really make a night of it.'

She grabbed his hand and dragged him down the stairs. 'It's Coney Island for you. I want to see you in the rolling pipes and if you don't get motion sickness I'm going to stick you to the wall in the Rotor.'

And the darkness was gone. Lifted from him by the light of her joy. He followed her, soaking in her delight in silly games, ridiculous rides and fairy floss. Her hand in his, laughing and looking at him to be sure he too enjoyed the night. A strange feeling to savour that she cared so much that he was the happy one.

He kissed her as she reached the end of the wacky walkway, kissed her after the slippery slide, and leant her back into the wall and kissed her thoroughly after another ride on the wild mouse.

The most memorable kiss—though not the most successful—was upside down in the centrifugal chamber where the forces glued them to the wall while the floor fell away. They only just made it back to upright before the floor came back and gravity returned.

From there it seemed natural to walk her back to his flat, hold her as they ascended the lift, and lean her against his outside wall while he opened the door.

Emily was in a fairy floss coloured daze. She hadn't laughed so much for years. She knew it wasn't real, it was all an illusion like the wacky mirrors that made you first fat and then thin. She was happy at this moment and she refused to look into the future and see the end of this night.

She'd never felt so silly, so beautiful, so protected. But she hadn't intended to come back to his flat. Tomorrow was a little too close for that.

And then they were inside and the door was shut. 'Now, how did I end up here?'

He watched her indulgently. Like she was a

child. She may have behaved like one but so had he. Make no mistake, though, she was a woman.

Marco said, 'It is your fault. You and your amusement parks exposing me to the testosterone of teenage boys and the flirtatiousness of a woman who could be a teenager herself.'

'I did not flirt.'

'Did you not? Then you were yourself. Incredible, whimsical, amazing self, and I am enthralled.'

She turned her back on him. Stared through the glass across the room at the harbour and thought of stopping this right here. Not taking this to the logical conclusion for a man of the world and a woman who had always wondered what good sex would be like.

She had to remember this man was heading off to the other side of the world very shortly. But maybe that was a good thing.

His arm dropped around her shoulders. 'Let us view the harbour.'

She glanced at his face. 'You didn't say come.'

'Perhaps later.'

CHAPTER FIVE

HE OPENED the sliding glass door and she went ahead to stand out on his terrace. A soft sea breeze ruffled her hair and he smoothed it with his hand.

The last few hours had tilted his axis. Twirled his thoughts like the rides had twirled their bodies, shifted his plans from conquest to surrender, made him see that taking this woman to bed when they had no future could harm her, and he didn't want to do that.

Soon he would move on to the next city. Needed to. Was unable to form a trusting relationship because so much trust had been broken in the past and the scars were deep. Had crippled him for the emotional agility a relationship needed.

But he wanted her badly.

She leaned back into his body, her slender neck enticing his mouth, and he dropped a kiss under her ear. She tasted so good, felt like silk, and her body pressed back into him so that they both felt his hardness rise.

She wriggled some more and he bit back a groan as he strove to speak normally. 'Perhaps we should go in. Would you like coffee?'

'It's not coffee I was thinking about.'

'Really?' His mind was lost to conversation. Was fixated on the woman in his arms. The need to create distance fading as the heat built between them.

He spoke into her hair. Desperate for one of them to be sensible. 'I leave in a few weeks. I may not return.'

She spun in his arms and looked up at him.

Unflinching. So courageous. Her head up. Green eyes burning like the starboard lights of ships in the night and he'd never wanted another woman more than at this moment when she offered herself to him.

Then unexpectedly she said, 'I'm a little rusty so you'd better be good.'

And his heart cracked open just a little more. He couldn't help the smile that pulled his cheeks and made him shake his head in wonder. Feel the pound of his heart and the jump in his groin.

'I am good.' Marco closed his arms around her and Emily's silver shoes left the ground.

Suddenly she was trembling with her own audacity but it felt so good. So different from going home alone tonight and regret and an empty bed.

He spun her like she'd been spun so many times in the last two hours and the lights of the harbour blurred as he swept through the doors with her hard against his chest, carried like a child, placed her like a princess in the middle of a gorgeously pillowed bed.

She watched him and he watched her. Pulled off his shoes and socks, unbuttoned his shirt, never taking his eyes from her face, until the shirt fell open to reveal the breadth of his chest, undid his trousers so that they flapped open to reveal the curling hairs that snaked down, slid them off to reveal his black briefs. Then he stopped.

She moistened her lips. Oh, my goodness. He was the most beautiful man she'd ever seen. In black shorts, just like she'd imagined. Her throat closed and she swallowed to moisten her dry mouth. 'I had hoped you might wear those black trunk things.'

'So you wondered.' He smiled at her and never had he looked more like the gypsy king as he did then with his dark chocolate eyes burning down at her. Just one word as he held out his hand.

'Come.'

And suddenly it was easy. To reach and take his hand. To stand in front of him as he undid the covered buttons on her blouse until it too hung open. Allow his big hands to slowly slide over her hips until she stood before him in her underwear. The only indulgence she allowed herself.

The tip of one long finger slid slowly from her throat, between her lace-covered breasts, to the top of her ribboned bikini. 'What is this delight?'

She blushed. Her secret was out but she doubted he'd be telling anybody. He'd better not.

'Such beautiful underclothes.' He brushed her face with his lips and bent to breathe his way down between her breasts. Tasting and murmuring. 'Such a beautiful body.' He looked up at her. 'You are exquisite.'

She should be doing something. Touching him, but she didn't know where to start. Shouldn't be just having all the fun. Tried not to look at the bulge in the dark briefs in front of her. She hadn't thought this far. To her inexperience. Her shortcomings as a lover. She could feel the beginnings of shame, left over from her rigid upbringing, left over from the horror of coldness and disgust from her parents the last time she'd lived with them.

She turned her head. She didn't want to think of that. Especially now.

Marco felt the change come over her. Looked swiftly at her face, straightened and drew her against him.

'What is it, *innamorata*? Sweetheart?'

'Nothing. Kiss me.'

It was not nothing. But he would kiss her. Hold her and show her how much he wanted her. And that was all for the moment. It would be no good for him if she was not also transported.

* * *

Emily sat in the pre-dawn light on the ferry huddled into her thin wrap, lost and confused, unable to believe she'd slept with him. While her daughter lay in hospital.

She'd woken at five, spooned by a strong man's body, the curve of her hips tucked into his heat, her lower body pleasantly aware of a new set of muscles she hadn't used in a while and her face had flamed as erotic snapshots of their night had blown on the embers low in her belly and urged her to arch back into him.

His arm had lain heavy across her shoulders as the panic had flared. Somewhere behind the panic a little voice had whispered that no wonder this golden man was sleeping like the dead. He was right. He was good.

She'd fought to keep her movements smooth as she'd eased out from under his hand and away from his body.

He'd murmured something in his sleep and

she'd pushed a pillow into his seeking hand and he'd drifted off again.

Scooped her bra from the floor and clipped it, she remembered that spot, had picked up her panties from the chair and pulled them on, and then her skirt and blouse. She'd glanced away from the chair, remembered Marco pulling her down onto his lap, and hurriedly scooped her shoes from under the bed—she certainly remembered the bed—and then she was dressed and couldn't think past the concept that she'd been the easiest conquest in the world.

So she'd let herself out, putting her silver shoes on in the hallway, and had tapped the lift button impatiently in case he opened the door.

Now here she was. Alone, shivering, pulling into her wharf in the early morning for the first time in her life that wasn't because of work.

An awful thought jolted as the ferry bumped the wharf and she checked her phone. No missed calls from Annie or the hospital. She sighed and thought self-mockingly, How lucky, because she suspected there had been some moments there when the whole apartment block could have come down around their ears and neither would have noticed. Would have thought it just part of the impact of making love together. Oh, my goodness, she wasn't sure how she could regret that!

Marco woke to an empty bed. Like he did every morning, because he never asked a woman to stay. Today he had expected it to be different.

He'd heard the door shut and he opened his eyes as he sighed, slapped his forehead, and groaned. What had he done? What had she done to him? His hand slid across the remaining warmth where her head had lain and he wanted to run. He just wasn't sure if it was as far as he could get from Sydney or after Emily.

He did neither. He sat on his terrace and nursed his espresso as he looked over the waking harbour. Imagined her hunched in the ferry on her way home, but by the time he realised she would be cold in her thin wrap it was too late to do anything but abuse his own stupidity.

Obviously she didn't want to face him this morning, which was a damn shame because already he missed her. Missed her in more ways than he should. Regretted, of course, they had not made love one more time—because he was afraid he hadn't quite got her out of his system. In fact, he regretted he hadn't the chance to share breakfast, drink coffee, watch boats together.

He missed her. Missed Emily. And this was bad for a man who did not wish to stay in one place.

CHAPTER SIX

'HI, MUM.' It was ten o'clock and Annie looked rosy cheeked and relaxed.

Unlike Emily, who could barely meet her daughter's eyes. 'You look good. How's your tummy this morning?'

'Not sore at all.' Annie stroked her little belly mound. 'And she's moving well. You look a little stressed. Stop worrying about us. We'll be fine.'

Oh, goodness. 'It's hard not to.' More guilt. 'But I'll try.' Emily looked across at June, because she didn't know what else to say. This was ridiculous. She needed to get a grip. No one was going to know and she could just push last night to the back of her head and forget it. Ha!

'Hi, there, June. How are you?'

'I'm good, thanks, Emily. How cool that Annie and I are roommates.'

'I know. That's great. You'll have to tell her about the calm breathing course you did.'

'I will.' June's mobile phone buzzed and Emily smiled and turned back to her daughter.

Annie whispered, 'She knows you're not going to go mad on her for the mobile phone. We try not to let the other staff see us use them.'

Emily lowered her own voice. 'Maternity's fine. We're separate from the rest of the hospital over the sky bridge and the high-tech equipment. It's easier for the staff too rather than running portable phones everywhere. They won't mind.'

Of course Annie had never been on this part of the hospital as a patient and her mother hadn't thought to explain yesterday. Was that because she'd been thinking of other things? Other people? A particular person?

Annie looked relieved. 'Oh, good. I'm almost out of credit. Can you get some, please?'

'I think they sell phone credit at the kiosk. I'll ask.'

'Goodie.' A word that reminded her how young Annie was. 'Do you know if Dr D'Arvello is coming in this morning?'

'It's Saturday.' Crikey, I hope not. Her neck heated. That was the reason she was here so early. It wasn't even visiting hours. 'Not sure. I'll just get that credit.'

She needed to get away for a minute and get her head together. She was a mess and she didn't like it. This was not how she did things. She was known for her calm and serene manner, famous for it over the hospital, and at the moment she couldn't even recognise herself.

Ten minutes later after her quick trip to the kiosk she was feeling calmer. Head down, she waited at the main lift as her mind sorted reasonable strategies for what she was going to say to Marco when she met him again.

Someone called her name. Twice. She looked up. Evie Lockheart stood next to her with a quizzical smile on her face. 'Earth to Emily?'

'Oh. Sorry. Hi, Evie. How are you?' She hadn't made that date for afternoon tea yet.

'So-so.' Evie frowned. 'You okay?'

'Yes.' Earth to Emily was right. She needed to plug into her surroundings. 'Of course. I'm visiting Annie. Her baby had intrauterine surgery yesterday.'

'Ah. I heard it all went well. Marco D'Arvello. Lucky we've got someone of his calibre here, even if it's for a short time.'

Emily nodded with her head down. 'He said Finn arranged his visit.'

'Finn likes him.'

Emily remembered yesterday in the cafeteria.

'Everything okay between you guys? I saw you in the kiosk yesterday.'

Evie shrugged. 'Ah. Yes. Well. He's a stubborn man.'

'I've heard men often are.'

Evie laughed. 'About time you did more than just hear that, isn't it?' Evie studied her face. 'Shouldn't you be retraining a stubborn man yourself?'

Marco wasn't stubborn. But she didn't say it. 'I'm a little snowed under with a pregnant daughter at the moment.'

'Of course. Though that's the funny thing about falling in love. It doesn't always pick the perfect moment to happen.'

Emily thought about that and didn't like the direction. 'Well, I'll be careful, then. This really isn't a good time for me to be sidetracked.' It wasn't too late!

The lift doors opened and they moved in.

Emily pressed sky bridge level and Evie leaned forward and pressed the button for Administration. The doors almost shut and then opened again.

Marco took two long strides from the left as the lift doors began to close. Stabbed the button. He'd seen Emily get in there. The doors re-opened and he stepped inside.

Her eyes widened and she stepped away from him back into the corner. This woman who had left his bed that morning. As if afraid of him?

A slice of pain he didn't expect. Did she feel she needed to do that? Peripherally he was aware there was another woman in the elevator so he leant against the side wall and nodded. It was the woman with Finn yesterday in the cafeteria.

The other woman smiled at him. 'We were just talking about you.' Vaguely he realised she was pretty but he only had eyes for Emily.

Then her words sank in. That wasn't what he

expected to hear. Gossip? He felt the air still in his lungs. Memories from his childhood as always the people whispered behind his back as he walked. Trust issues reared their ugly head. His father's words, 'Never trust anyone.' So already she was boasting. He had not expected that.

She held out her hand. 'I'm Evie Lockheart. So you operated on Annie yesterday.'

Ah. *'Si.'* They shook hands. 'Dr Lockheart. You must thank Finn for me. Last night we dined on the brig.' Then Evie's last words penetrated the haze of hurt. She'd only said he'd operated on her daughter.

Evie's face lit up. 'The three-master? Lovely. And the weather was great last night. Who'd you go with?'

Emily's face was pink and already he felt guilt for his thoughts—let alone the indiscretion he had started in retaliation. 'A friend.'

The lift stopped and the doors opened. Evie

turned to Emily, saw her red face and frowned, but Marco had his hand across the doors, waiting for her to exit. 'Is this you?'

She turned to look at him. Glanced at Emily again and stepped out. 'Thanks. See you later, Emily.'

'Bye, Evie.' Emily didn't step away from the corner as the lift doors closed.

Evie Lockheart watched the lift doors shut. Frowned. Stared at the doors a minute longer and then smiled. There just might be something going on there.

Nice if someone had a normal relationship. Emily deserved it. She turned and headed down to Finn's office. She hoped to hell he'd calmed down since yesterday.

Sometimes she felt as if she was just another conquest to him and at others she thought she glimpsed their unwilling connection. But, damn it, she cared.

He'd point blank refused to talk to her about his problem. Like the future of his career wasn't worrying him. She only wanted to help.

She'd been shocked by the depth of emotional turmoil she'd seen in his eyes. Finn the invincible looking just for a moment anything but invincible and it had stayed with her. Of course it had stayed with her. She'd barely slept. But then again she hadn't slept well since the day she'd gone to his flat and discovered a side to herself she hadn't realised existed. A wanton, wild and womanly side she'd only shown to Finn.

A side that he had mocked—and here she was, back for more.

But today wasn't about that—or even them as a couple, if that was what they were. It was to talk about the possibility of a cure. Again.

Yesterday's discussion hadn't worked. From

the little he had let drop, the experimental sur-gery—despite the huge risk—offered a chance Finn could continue the work he lived for and take away the pain he tried to hide. If it was a success.

Even odds. Fifty per cent he might be able to operate or fifty per cent he might never oper-ate again.

All this was constantly going over in her mind and how she could broach the subject when he obviously wanted no interference from her, and it was driving her bonkers. Unfortunately, she couldn't leave it alone.

Wouldn't leave Finn to go through this alone. She had to believe they had a connection and he was the one pretending they didn't.

She paused outside his office door and drew a deep breath. 'Gird your loins, girl,' she mocked herself. She knocked.

No answer. So she knocked again. 'Finn?'

Silence. She pushed open the door and the room was empty. Damn. She circled the empty room, frustration keeping her moving as she realised she'd have to psych herself up all over again. Then her gaze fell on his desk.

The research papers he'd mentioned. Explanations of the experimental surgery. So he had considered it, despite his horror of the risks. She could understand that, see his abhorrence of life without his work, but he had to do it. You couldn't live with increasing pain for ever. The time was past when he could do nothing.

'What are you doing here?' Finn stood tall and menacing in the doorway with blue ice shooting from his arctic eyes.

I'm not scared, she told herself, but she swallowed.

Guess he was still seething from yesterday, then. 'Waiting for you.'

'Why are you rifling my desk?'

She raised her eyebrows, outwardly calm. 'Hardly rifling when it was all open for me to see.'

He stepped into the room and the space around her shrank to a quarter of the size. Funny what the aura of some people could do. 'Not for you to see.'

Evie stood her ground. 'Afraid I might suggest you consider it again?' She paused. 'So at least you've read it?'

He ignored that. 'I've read it. And I don't want to talk about it.'

She stepped around the desk until she was standing beside him. This man who infuriated and inspired and drove her insane with frustration and, she had to admit, a growing love and need to see him happy.

'It's a choice, Finn. One you're going to have to consider.'

His voice grated harshly. His face was set like

stone. 'Now you want to look after me? One episode of good sex is all it took?'

She ignored that. Ignored the splinter of pain that festered inside from his contempt. Banished the pictures of him showing her the door afterwards.

'Hippocratic oath,' he mocked. 'Save your patient.'

'You're not my patient.' She met his eyes. Chin up. 'Just think about it.'

His eyes narrowed further. 'Why should you care?'

'Because I do.' She touched his arm and the muscles were bunched and taut beneath her fingers. 'Is that so hard to believe?'

He shook her off. 'I look after myself. Had to all my life and it's never going to change.'

She took his hand and held it firmly. Looked into his face. 'Tell me.'

He looked down but this time he didn't pull away. 'Tell you what?'

She shook his arm. 'Finn. For God's sake, let me in.' Finally he seemed to get it. A glimmer of understanding of what she wanted to know. Why she wanted to know.

'What?' A scornful laugh not directed at her for a change. 'The whole sob story?'

Evie didn't move. 'Yes. Please.'

He sighed. Her hand fell away as he turned and stared out over the harbour and when he started his voice was flat, emotionless, daring her to be interested in his boring tale. 'Why would you want this? You probably know most of it. Orphan. Unstable foster-homes. The army was my best parenting experience and they don't do affection or connection.'

A sardonic laugh that grated on her ears. 'Maybe that's why I fitted so well.'

She wanted to hug him. 'You did connection okay the other night.'

She saw his frown from across the room. 'Don't go there, Evie.' She flinched and he sighed. 'Do you want to hear or not?'

She held up her hands. 'Please.'

This time he turned to look at her fully and she watched the muscle jerk in his cheek as he held emotion rigidly in check. She wanted to cradle his head in her hands but she was too scared to interrupt him. Too scared she'd stop the flow she'd waited so long for him to start.

'You know about Isaac. I had to watch my brother die. The same bomb that tore into me, which is wrecking my career now, took his life. The day Isaac died I died too, Evie. Since then, what little ability I had to love, I lost. And with Isaac gone I lost the only person who really cared what happened to me.' He shrugged.

'That's why I am what I am. I don't want to be around someone when I feel like that.'

She took a step towards him. Aware how much it would hurt if at this moment he rebuffed her. 'You don't have to feel like that, Finn.'

Sardonic sweep of eyebrows. Daring her to contradict him. 'Don't I?'

'No.' Closer.

'Why's that, Evie?' The biting sarcasm was back but she refused to be put off by it. Toughened herself because she would never be cowed by this angry man who frightened others to keep them at bay.

Another step. 'I care what happens to you, Finn.'

Vehement shake of his head. 'Don't pity me, Evie.'

She almost laughed. 'You're not a man anyone can pity, Finn. You won't allow it. You alienate people so they don't. But unfortunately I feel so much more for you than that.'

She swallowed, tossed caution to the winds, stepped closer and stared into his face so he couldn't ignore her words. 'I love you, Finn Kennedy. And there's not a lot of reward for that at the moment.'

A more subtle shake of the head. 'How can you love me?'

Now she was in front of him again. 'How can I not, you stupid man? I think about you every minute of every day, wondering when you're going to care for yourself like you should.'

He sidestepped her, crossed the room to shut the door, shut out the hospital for probably the first time since he'd started here, and then came back. Put himself in her space deliberately.

'What are you saying, Evie?'

'I love you. Foul temper and all.'

His hands slid around her waist. 'I didn't ask

for that.' Something in his voice had changed. Gave her a glimmer of hope.

'You didn't ask for it?' She stared into the harsh and haunted face she loved so much. 'Neither did I. But there's not a lot we can do about it now.'

His face softened just a little. 'So you weren't just after sex the other day?'

This was what she dreaded. 'What do you think, Finn? Did it feel like that to you?' She'd laid herself open, exposed her soft underbelly of caring, and he could mortally wound her, even worse than he had after she'd given herself to him.

He lifted his hand and stroked the hair out of her eyes. 'No.' He sighed. 'Though God knows why you bother. What I felt the other day scared the hell out of me, Evie. And that's not all I'm scared of. I'm scared I'm not the man you think I am.'

'Well, seeing that I don't want to be without you, Finn, we'll just have to take that chance. Whatever happens, I'm here for you. And always will be.'

He shook his head. Couldn't accept that. 'I might not just be an emotional cripple, Evie. I could be in a wheelchair.'

She leaned towards him. 'Or it could be the answer to all your medical problems. You could get full control back. You have to take that chance.'

'I don't think it's an option.' He sighed. 'But I'll think about it.' An air of finality.

She had to be satisfied with that. It was better than they'd had before today.

CHAPTER SEVEN

THE lift doors closed after Evie left and the silence deepened with Marco and Emily alone in the lift.

Finally. 'I'm sorry.' Marco sighed as the elevator began its ascent. 'I thought you had spoken about our evening out with her.'

And, boy, were you unhappy! 'I gathered that.' So he was that embarrassed to say he'd taken her out. Not that she wanted to be the centre of a gossip storm.

She went on, 'You were pretty quick to retaliate.' Like a cobra, and a big warning for the future. Or their lack of it.

'My apologies. Again.' His face stayed frozen

and even his words seemed to have difficulty leaving his mouth. 'It is how I am.'

He must have an interesting history—but she wasn't going there. Emily sighed. So he hated gossip. She did too.

But they were both mad if they thought the whole hospital wouldn't find out anyway. It always happened. She'd seen it time and again over the last sixteen years.

Somebody's son would be a waiter on the boat or a deckhand on the ferry. A woman thought nobody knew and usually she was the last to figure out everyone had been talking about her for a week. Now she'd be one of those. Thanks, Marco.

And a bit of ill feeling might help keep him at bay. Maybe cultivating that wasn't a bad idea. 'As long as we don't repeat the experience, I'm sure we'll both be fine.'

He stepped across to her. 'And yet I'd hoped

to see you again, spend more time with you be-fore I spoiled my chance.'

'No. Thank you, Marco. You're not my favour-ite person at the moment.'

The lift stopped and he moved back as the doors opened. Emily didn't look at him as she left but she could feel him behind her as she walked towards the nurses' station.

Then he was gone as she went on to Annie's room.

When he walked in five minutes later Emily had herself well in hand. She smiled distantly at his left shoulder, watched her daughter's face the whole time, and agreed that tomorrow morning would be a good time to pick Annie up.

Then he was behind the curtain, talking to June, and she could drop the silly smile from her face and get on with life.

'You okay, Mum?'

She jumped. Annie was staring at her. 'Sorry? Oh. Yes. Fine. I'm tired.'

'Didn't you sleep last night?'

There was silence from behind the curtain. Maybe he was just feeling June's tummy. 'Oh. Um. Not as well as I'd hoped.'

Conversation started behind the curtain and she frowned at herself. Stop it.

'Why don't you stay home this afternoon? Just chill. I'm fine. Some friends are coming in to see me in visiting hours and I have my phone credit now. I can ring if I want anything.'

And do what? Mope? 'No. Don't be silly. I'll come back this afternoon.'

'Seriously, Mum. I'm just as happy if you don't.'

She looked at Annie. Hurt. Stung and embarrassed that everyone else in the room would have heard it too.

'Oh. Okay. That sounds fine, then.' Ridiculous

stinging in her eyes and she'd be mortified if she cried. 'I'll catch up on all the things I've been meaning to do.' Forced brightness. 'Lovely.'

She leant over and kissed her daughter's cheek. Avoided her eyes but, then, Annie seemed to be avoiding hers too. Maybe she realised she'd been an ungrateful little wretch. Wishful thinking probably. She had her friends coming. She didn't need a mother. 'See you tomorrow.'

She walked hurriedly away but not hurriedly enough. Marco caught up with her in four strides. 'Are you okay?'

She paused, turned and stared at his tie. 'Fine. I'm sorry. Perhaps we were both rude in the lift. Thanks for last night.'

Then she walked away. Thanks for last night? She winced. What did she mean? Dinner. Great sex. Today was a difficult day but she'd got through others.

She could feel his eyes on her back.

She wasn't surprised when he turned up at her house two hours later. He was bearing gifts. Well, food anyway.

She stood back to let him enter. 'I guess we do need to talk.' A lingering trail of subtle exotic herbs and spices followed him.

'And I wish to apologise again.'

What was in that bag? 'For what?'

'For my comment in the elevator. For doubting you.'

She forgot food and studied him. He had his mask face on again and she wondered where the smiling Italian gypsy had gone. But, then, again the smiling Emily seemed a tad AWOL at the moment as well. 'Why are you here, Marco?' Because I don't want to fall for you.

'To see you. To ask why you left this morning. To see if you are all right because I have been worried I made you unhappy.'

'You don't have to worry about me. I'm a big girl.' Better on my own.

'Last night at the fair you worried about my happiness.'

'Last night was an illusion.' She sighed. 'A really fun one but still an illusion. Look, Marco. You're a great guy. Too great. And I haven't got the best track record in not falling for the wrong guys. You're leaving in three weeks and I don't want to get any more used to you being around. It's too good. So there won't be any repeats.'

'What about lunch?' He glanced at his parcel.

'No.'

'Please?'

She couldn't throw him out. 'Lunch I could probably manage but only because I need to know what that incredible smell is coming from those bags.'

He obliged in relief. 'Let me show you.'

'That's what you said last night.' She flicked a

look at him from under her lashes and the other man was back.

Emily sighed because she knew she was in trouble. 'Come through to the kitchen.' It was just too hard to maintain distance when he was grinning and producing delicacies like rabbits from a hat.

'*Si.* The rolls are crusty, the butter fresh churned, and many cheeses.' He pulled out some plastic takeaway containers and she realised the aroma came from there.

'Fresh sage?'

'No festive Tuscan meal would be complete without chicken liver crostini.'

'We're not having a party.'

'It is Saturday. We should. *Crostini di Fegatini di Pollo.*' Emily wasn't really sure she could eat liver.

As if he'd read her mind. 'Even those who dislike liver enjoy this on thinly cut crusty bread. Trust me.'

That was what it all boiled down to, she thought glumly. Trust him. Or trust herself. If either of them dropped control, she doubted trust would have a look in.

He pulled out a dish of pasta. She could see mushrooms and red peppers, could smell the provolone cheese and the basil. It made her mouth water and he saw. He smiled.

'We will have a picnic in your tiny back yard. Perhaps you could lay the table and I will serve these.'

So now he was ordering her around in her own kitchen. Was opening and shutting Gran's cupboards as he looked for dishes to serve from. She couldn't take it all in. Was bemused by his energy and sudden good humour and becoming fixated on the way his shoulders moved and his biceps flexed as he reached for highly placed articles.

Might be best to leave him to it and grab a checked tablecloth and some cutlery and bolt outside.

The air cooled her cheeks. It was a glorious day. Funny she hadn't noticed that this morning. Not too hot. Outside anyway.

She glanced over her shoulder and he was singing in her kitchen. She'd never heard a man singing baritone in her kitchen before and she paused as the sound teased her. Made her smile. Chased away caution again because, darn it, it was good to have so much fun.

She set the table with new vigour, wondered about that bottle of cold Chablis she had in the fridge, and a rainbow lorikeet flew down and scratched in the empty bird feeder and then glared at her.

'Okay. Okay. I'll get some.' Gran had always

fed the lorikeets. It was a bit early in the afternoon for this bloke but maybe he was having a bad day. She could relate to that.

She almost walked into Marco and he put his hands out to steady her. 'Who are you talking to?'

'The lorikeet is complaining there's no seed.' She tried not to stare at his chest but it filled her vision. She wanted to bury her nose in him. 'Do you need something?'

'Glasses. I brought Lambrusca.'

All she could think of was how good his hands felt on her arms. 'Aren't you driving?' No matter she'd been going to offer him white wine.

'Not yet, and we can have a glass. You keep the rest.'

'Trying to loosen my morals again?' She stepped past him and his hands fell.

'There is nothing wrong with your morals, Emily. I look forward to sharing your lunch.'

That had been rude. She turned back. 'Sorry. I'm not good at this.' Then she disappeared into the kitchen.

Marco watched her go. She was very good at this. He was a mess.

He didn't follow. Gave her a moment to gather her composure. He should not have come but had been unable to stay away. He should know better.

He stared at the brilliantly coloured bird on the steel feeder, iridescent red and lime green and vibrant yellow all mixed in the lorikeet's plumage as if painted by a colour-hungry child. So much of this country was bright and brash and brilliant so it hurt your eyes.

There might be more pain in store for him here. Seeing Emily's pain hurt his eyes and his heart when she was upset and his stomach when she was away from him. He should go in and help her bring the food out.

She reappeared before he could move. 'I've brought the wine out. It looks good.'

'And for after... Limoncello.' He wondered if she'd like the liqueur and looked forward to her reaction. 'Nectar of the gods. I will help you carry the rest.'

Soon they were seated, shaded by the tree that hung over the fence from next door, and Marco felt a peace settle over him that defied description and warned him to be careful.

'Gran always said that tree was the best of both worlds. The trunk didn't take up any room in our yard and we got the shade.'

He glanced up at the thick, glistening foliage. Little brown birds flitted around in it. 'Tell me about your gran. Was she a widow?'

'My grandfather died in the Vietnam War. His family owned this whole block all the way down to the water. There's a magnificent old home over that fence and this was the dower house.

The big house left the family years ago and this little house was left to my gran, and I always think of her here.'

He glanced around and the feeling of peace deepened. 'No doubt she is here.'

'I'd like to think so.'

He smiled. 'My grandmother came from a long line of gypsies and we can tell these things. This tiny house is very beautiful and full of character. Like its mistress now, and no doubt also the one from the past.'

'Thank you, Marco. That's a lovely thing to say.' She tilted her head. 'So tell me about the gypsies?'

His peace seeped away. Serve him right. 'There's not much to tell. My father was not one, yet still we moved a lot.'

She put her chin in her hands. A willing listener eager to hear his exotic tales. 'It sounds very romantic.'

She would be disappointed. 'I can assure you it was not.'

'So what made you want to become a doctor?'

Marco shook his head and realised it would take more to daunt this woman or her curiosity. He owed her a little more than he usually gave.

Why had he become a doctor? Many reasons, but the need had been strong enough to drive him along the hard road his career had carried him. He tried to verbalise it. 'To help others? To stretch my brain. To find solutions to pain. Perhaps a need to feel worthwhile.'

She frowned. Stretched her hand across and took his. Lifted his palm and placed a kiss in his hand as a gift. 'Worthwhile doesn't even begin to describe you and your work.'

Her words made his heart ache and he tried to harden himself against her. As if she knew, she shook her head. 'All those babies, parents, grandparents who needed your help. Families like us. Like June.'

He shrugged. 'Everyone does their part.'

She squeezed his hand and then let him go. 'And some strive to achieve the impossible when others fear to push boundaries.' She shrugged and smiled at her seriousness.

'But I see this isn't helping your mood so instead we will toast.'

She glanced around for inspiration and he watched her eyes light up with amusement. Up went his own spirits.

'To lorikeets, and harbour boats and wild mice.'

'Especially wild mice.' She captivated him. 'I will certainly toast that.' He smiled. 'And I am partial to the idea of your rotor. Cannot help but wonder what could be achieved without the benefit of gravity.'

She blushed and concentrated on her antipasto. 'See. No fear to push boundaries.'

He laughed and they ate and sipped and laughed again until the afternoon shade brought a chill and they cleared up their picnic together.

The kitchen was small, and smaller still as Marco dried the dishes while she washed, and Emily tried hard not to bump into him. Every time she did, awareness grew, every 'Excuse me' made her mouth dry as she reached past, and gradually the laughter of the lunch changed to a slowly rising tension that burned in the pit of her belly and warned her of imminent danger.

Glances collided, hands brushed, and as the last dish dried Emily's nerves screamed to create some distance or give in.

In the end, Marco took her shoulders and held her. Stared down with those dark eyes, like the coffee she'd made that still sat on the bench. 'It is not coffee I want, Emily.'

Emerrrleee. She savoured the sound of her name on his lips again. Relished the power in his hands as he held her. Acknowledged the lust that rose like a wraith inside her. She wanted him too.

His hand brushed her cheek. She stepped closer. That was all the permission he needed and once more she was swept up. Spun in the confines of the kitchen, carried across and under the arch into the hall, and in through the door to her bedroom.

She let her head fall back. Closed her eyes. Acknowledged the surge of power she felt to ignite his passion and accept her femininity. She was a woman. She did have needs. And she wanted Marco so badly the centre of her being ached with that need.

Then he placed her on her bed. Gently. And stepped back. 'Perhaps this time you would like to undress me?'

She raised her eyebrows. 'Mmm.' She crawled off the bed, accentuating the wiggle of her bottom, and his voice deepened with amusement and definite intent.

'Although if you persist with that movement, you will not have the chance.'

She stood up. Sidled up to him. Ran her finger down his chest and he laughed with delight. 'I have created a monster.'

'You have no idea.'

Marco was dazed. Stunned and enthralled by the sexy innocent who had suddenly shed her shyness and had taken control. It was dream and fantasy and to think that she could trust him enough to allow her playful side to surface when she had been so hurt in the past.

She ran her hands down each side of the buttons on his shirt, feeling his chest, until they dipped under his belt. Deftly undoing the buckle, she opened the top button of his trousers and he couldn't help the sigh of relief at the extra room afforded.

Then she flitted back to the neck of his shirt. Skipping from button to button, a kiss for each opening, a kiss down his chest until the last button ended back at his trousers. She looked up at him. Mischief, and still that tiny hint of vulnerability, and suddenly he could not take any more of this.

He captured her face in his hands. Drew her up until he could reach those perfect lips, hugged her against him, then in a flurry their clothes were slipping from their bodies with minds of their own. He could only see Emily. Her face, her mouth and her truth shining out at him.

He thanked her in the only way he knew how. With reverence at first and then with mounting passion, mutual need creating a maelstrom that seemed to intensify each time he joined with this woman.

CHAPTER EIGHT

THIS time when she woke she knew her survival depended on not seeing this man again. But she had the horrible feeling it was too late.

And this time it was Marco who was leaving. He turned when she stirred. Strode back to the bed fully dressed. Kissed her one last time, thoroughly, and stroked her face. 'I must go. *Ciao, bella.*' And left.

'*Ciao.* Bye.' She didn't ask why he had to go. She had an idea. This connection, rapport, infatuation, whatever they were going to call it, had been more than either of them had expected. And he was leaving at the end of the month. Not the most sensible thing to continue.

She rose, wandered into the shower, dressed again

and tidied the wreckage of her bedroom. She had to smile. With a slightly embarrassed smugness. He'd said he was good. Judging by his response, she was a fast learner.

Marco had had to get out. He'd been a fool. Did he think that reciting the reasons he was a loner would be good enough to insulate him from falling for Emily? He was no long-term prospect for any woman, let alone one as special as this woman, and his gut had told him that from the first day.

He needed to leave. Move on. Needed to keep presenting his best side to the world and avoid the chance others would find out that he was irrevocably tainted by his dubious background and should never be trusted. He didn't trust himself.

Look what he had done to Emily.

He had seen the light in her eyes when she'd looked at him. No doubt that same light had shone from his own stupid face. *Bastardo.* He was as bad as her daughter's father. But he had been unable to back away when he should have. Had been seduced when he was the one who normally did the seducing. She was incredible.

He parked his car in the garage and took the stairs to his unit, changed quickly, and left again. He needed exercise. He needed to drive himself to exhaustion. He needed to run until he dropped. Run until his legs ached and his head drooped. Run until he could forget that he was tempted to risk all and even think about a life that existed in one city with one woman.

Emily had to get out of the house. She stared at herself in the hall mirror. Her eyes shone, her face gently glowed and a small smile tilted her mouth even when she tried to look serious. 'I'm falling in love and I can't. He's transient,' she told the mirror. 'He's going to leave me, like Annie's father left me. Though, to be fair, Marco had always said he wasn't planning on staying.'

She sighed. 'What is it about me that men don't want to stay around?'

Maybe Annie would welcome her for a short time. She winced at this morning's hurt at her daughter's dismissal. Well, she was always there for Annie and right at this moment her mother needed her.

She glanced at the grandmother clock on the wall. It was almost the end of visiting hours. She could take an ice cream, sit with her daughter for the last fifteen minutes. Then maybe she would be able to come home and settle for an early night. She started her week of night duty again tomorrow night so it was important she feel refreshed before the new week began.

Refreshed? She felt like she'd been plugged into a power source. 'If that's what sex does for you, my battery must have been low for years,' she muttered to herself as she locked the door behind her.

When Emily walked into Annie's room in the hospital a little later, at first glance she thought she'd taken the wrong doorway. The woman on the bed was wrapped in the arms of a dark-haired tattooed boy and their absorption in each other forcibly reminded her of what she'd been doing earlier in the day.

'Ahem...' She cleared her throat, and the couple on the bed jumped apart. No mistake on the room number, then.

'Mum!'

'Annie.' She waited.

'Um. This is Rodney.' Annie looked at the young man and lifted her chin. 'My baby's father.'

Tattoos. Undernourished. Torn jeans. Emily tried not to cry. 'Hello, Rodney. Nice to meet you.' She paused. 'At last.' Very dry.

Rodney stood up awkwardly. Wiped his palms on his jeans and held out his hand.

Emily forced a smile and shook. 'So is this an unexpected reunion or the reason I wasn't supposed to visit today?'

'Um. Hello, Mrs...Miss...' He glanced agonisingly at Annie, and then struggled on manfully, 'Emily. I'm sorry we haven't met before.' He sent one last agonising look at Annie. 'I—I have to go.' And hurried from the room.

Marco stepped out of the lift as a young man, his face painfully red from embarrassment, hurried past. *Christo.* He remembered that feeling. Unworthy. Scorned by someone he wanted to impress. Too many times this had happened to him at his age. He wanted to take the boy aside and tell him he must love himself before others could love him. But for all his efforts he had never learned that lesson. He shook his head and walked on to the nurses' station, the memories circling like bats around his head. Work. He needed work.

In Annie's room the young girl sat higher in the bed. 'Look what you did.' She adjusted her pyjamas and glared at her mother.

Good grief, times had changed, Emily thought. Imagine if she'd said that to *her* mother. 'I'm sorry. I don't understand? What I did?'

Annie crossed her arms over her chest. 'You made him leave.'

'Not guilty.' Emily held up her hands. 'I did no such thing. Not my fault Rodney didn't want to stay while I was here.'

Annie fumed. 'You shouldn't have been here. I asked you not to come.'

Emily took a step closer to the bed. The idea of a cosy chat with her daughter, a mutual salve for unstable times, lay in tatters around her feet.

'You said friends. When were you going tell me you were seeing your baby's father again? You went behind my back. Sneakily. Annie? Where has all this come from?'

Annie glanced away. 'I knew you'd judge him just because he doesn't come from a good family.'

Emily shook her head. 'That's unfair. Since when have I *ever*—' she stressed the 'ever' '—tried to influence your choice of friends?'

'I know what you're thinking, Mum!' Annie's voice rose.

Marco paused outside the room. Unwilling to interrupt when he was obviously not wanted but unable to avoid the conversation.

'I know how you looked at Rodney. As if he's not good enough for me.'

Emily's voice. Quieter. Calm. 'That's unfair.'

'He's tainted by a family that doesn't live in the

best part of Sydney. Doesn't work all day.' A bitter pause then a little softer and Marco tried not to strain his ears. 'Or all night, like you.' Ouch.

Annie went on, 'I know it's going to be because his brother's done time.' Marco straightened as if stung.

'Jail?' The horror in Emily's voice said it all. Did it all. Sealed it all. Marco sighed. Pictured that boy's face. Empathised. Felt the whoosh of time, of scornful villagers, of police questioning. He winced and walked away. And to think he had considered telling Emily about his past. About his reasons for choosing not to settle. Why? Did he hope she would not care? Fool.

He knew exactly what she was thinking. Of course. And he didn't blame her. Marco kept walking. Each step to the lift more final with his decision. He would stay away. Not seek out Emily. He had done enough damage. He would just do his work and then leave.

He pressed the lift button. Stepped inside, saw little, had trouble deciding on the floor he wanted and totally oblivious to the other occupant.

'What are you doing here today?' A gruff masculine voice.

He looked up. Hard blue eyes scrutinised him. Finn Kennedy. He was rubbing his shoulder.

'Just checking on my patients. You?' Ball back in Finn's court because his mind wasn't working real well at the moment. He'd been delusional to think he could just have fun with Emily.

'Same.' Finn nodded. 'Want a drink?'

Emily was trying to make sense of it all. Of this woman who was and yet wasn't her daughter. 'What do you mean done time? Rodney?'

'See. I knew it. It's not Rodney's fault his brother made mistakes. Rodney's had a difficult life but he is still a good man.'

'Annie.' She sat on the edge of the bed. 'I don't care what Rodney's family have done. What Rodney's background is. It's what he himself is doing with his life now and that he makes you happy that I care about. That he loves you and your baby. Treats you both right. Every woman and every child deserves that.'

Annie's lip quivered. 'I thought you'd look down on him because of his brother's past; you think I'd be tied for ever to a family of trouble.'

'Why? How could I do that?' She shook her head. 'Your father was from a very well-to-do family. An upstanding future citizen. Once a year his parents send money, sure—but he dropped me, and you, like a hot potato.'

She patted Annie's hand. 'Your father never visited me in hospital like Rodney has visited you. Why would you think I'd look down on that?' Her voice firmed. 'But if Rodney ever treated you badly then he'd have me after him.'

Annie shrugged. 'If he treated me badly, I wouldn't be there.'

'That's my girl.'

They looked at each other and then Annie held out her arms for a hug. 'I'm sorry, Mum. I should have told you.'

Emily hugged her and Annie squeezed back. 'Is this why we've been fighting the last few months?'

Annie nodded. 'I hated having a secret and I should have known you'd understand.'

Emily swallowed the thickness in her throat. Maybe she'd have her normal daughter back now. She glanced down at the plastic bag on the table. 'Now I have two melted ice creams we were going to share because I got lonely and needed my baby's company.'

She pulled out a droopy ice cream and gave it

to Annie. Annie looked at it, took it gingerly and stripped it of its wrapper. She grinned. It didn't quite fall off the stick. 'I'm sorry.'

'That's fine.' Emily pulled hers out and it looked worse. They both giggled.

Emily pulled the towel off the end of the bed and spread it between them as a safety net for dripping ice cream. 'I guess I have to realise you won't be there for ever. You have your own life. But when you're ready I need you to tell me about Rodney and what your plans are.'

'There's not much to tell. I love him.'

Emily's brows went up. 'Really. Where did you meet him? How long have you known him? Though I'm guessing more than twenty-six weeks?'

'Mum!'

Emily raised her brows and glanced at Annie's belly. 'Well?'

'I met him in a chat room. Just after Gran died.

And before you go, "Oh, Annie", it's okay. We'd been chatting for about three months before I met him, and we can talk all night. He understands me, likes the same things—music, books, movies. We laugh. A lot. And when I met him...' Annie rolled her eyes '...it was just right.'

'Okay. I can understand that.' Boy, could she understand that. 'But did you mean to have a baby with Rodney? I mean, how old is he?'

'Eighteen. And no. We only did it once. And we weren't going to do it again until I went on the Pill. But when I finally went to the doctor he told me I was pregnant.'

Oh, my poor baby. 'We must be very fertile women.' That thought came with a shudder of relief that she'd started the Pill after Annie's birth and never missed it. So she could banish the horrible vision of the two of them eating ice creams with pregnant bellies. And Marco had been careful too.

Emily accepted how it had happened. 'Though for the record, if you like a boy enough to want to have sex, it would be good to let me into the secret so I could at least meet him. When all this is over, we're going to discuss contraception again.'

Annie blushed. 'It's a bit late now.'

'Not for the next one it's not.' And if she could cover herself for the last sixteen years and not use it, her daughter would be doubly covered. 'And condoms.'

'Mu-u-um.' Annie rolled her eyes again.

She grinned. 'Sorry. Having a belated stress attack. This has all happened pretty fast, you know.'

Annie's fingers crept across and squeezed her mother's hand. 'I know. And I'm sorry. I've been crabby because I was hiding Rodney and it felt rotten to be sneaky.'

'You didn't need to do that. You can always

tell me anything. I may not like it but I'll always love you.'

Annie sighed. 'Rodney wanted to. He wanted to drive around to home and be with me when I told you. But I didn't want you to meet him for the first time then.'

Emily felt her heart squeeze. Wished for a different scenario, but it was all too late now. 'You'll have to grow up too fast. But we'll talk more about that later.' She glanced at her watch. 'Visiting hours are over. I'd better go.'

Annie reached out her hand. 'Mum?'

Emily stopped. 'Yes?' She caught her daughter's hand and held it.

'Can we put your birthday decorations up when I come home?'

Emily squeezed Annie's hand. 'Sure. I'd like that.'

Annie hung on for another second. 'And thanks for the ice cream.'

'Thanks for the conversation.' Their hands dropped apart. 'I've missed having them with you.'

They hugged again because they were both a little teary as they waved goodbye.

Marco hunched over his beer at Pete's Bar, a watering place across the road from the hospital where most of the staff drifted if they didn't want to be alone—or wanted to be alone in a section Pete called Off Limits.

The aroma of beef pie permeated the walls and Pete himself remembered every name he was told. He had twenty years of hospital names stored in his head.

Finn ordered the pie. 'You should try it. To die for.'

Marco looked at it consideringly. 'I have eaten but maybe I could manage one. I think I ran that off.' And some other exercise, he reminded himself sardonically.

'Evie says you're seeing Emily Cooper.'

His appetite disappeared. So she had told her in the lift. And he'd apologised. Before he could say anything, Finn went on. 'Good woman. Good midwife in an emergency too. Not the kind I would have thought up for a fling.'

'We went out once.' And slept together twice.

Finn looked at him under his brows. Must have seen something in his face. 'Emily hasn't said anything. Evie said she was in the lift with you two and could've cut the air with a knife.'

He'd got it wrong, again. Suspicion would kill him one day. 'Very observant of her. I think I will have the pie.' He stood up and walked over to the bar to order.

Man after his own heart. 'Use your staff card. It's half price,' Finn called out, suddenly in a good humour because he'd found some other poor bastard who didn't understand women either.

There was a lot of Marco D'Arvello that reminded Finn of Isaac. His brother had had that same kindness and warm exterior, and Finn wondered if Marco hid a similar feeling of homelessness. Thankfully Isaac had found happiness for the time he'd had with his wife, Lydia, something Finn had never allowed himself to find. The closest he'd come had been when he and Lydia had comforted each other after Isaac's death. Lydia had been smart enough to know there was no future with Finn.

But now there was Evie. The reason he'd decided to come across here and think. That and the pain that was eating him alive.

Headstrong, defiant, warm-hearted Evie who for some incomprehensible reason said she loved him and he couldn't quite believe it.

That was the problem. He didn't want to risk

becoming a quadriplegic—or worse—if she was going to hang her future on him. But there was the chance this surgery could remove the shrapnel and give him back full control of his hands.

Did he owe it to Evie to try? Or owe it to Evie to be half a man instead of just a shell? If he chose the surgery he'd just have to make a backup plan to get away if it all went wrong.

'You okay? You look worried. What's up?' Marco was back and he could see Finn was in pain. He set the pie down.

'Nothing.' Subject change. 'So you're leaving in a couple of weeks?'

'Is it that close?' Marco shrugged. 'Doesn't matter. You want to roster me on?' He tried not to think of Emily. Of her character-filled house. Her family. He didn't do families.

Of course Finn jumped at the offer. 'The O and G guys would be thrilled. It's always a pain getting cover.'

'Fine.' So this was penance. He could have left Sydney in fourteen days. 'But I wish to be gone by the twentieth.'

'Planning something special?'

He said the first thing that appeared in his mind. 'Times Square.' He'd be in New York for the new contract but it was unlikely he'd be out partying.

'So, you going out with Emily again?' Finn's curiosity surprised him. Marco had never known him to be interested in someone else's social life. Perhaps his friend was becoming more human.

'I doubt it. She has a lot on her mind with her daughter.'

'It's a big responsibility. She does seem fairly consumed by her. I wouldn't like to have a teenage daughter. Especially a pregnant one.'

'Emily is a good mother.'

'No doubt about that but she wouldn't know

squat about teenage boys and that's how their life is going to change.'

Marco thought about that. Thought about the young man he'd seen. Emily's natural reservations. About who was going to help her? And maybe the boy?

CHAPTER NINE

EMILY walked onto the ward Monday morning to collect Annie and the dull ache behind her eyes wasn't helped when she saw Marco was still there.

'Ah. Here is your mother.' His glance swept over her. No doubt he could see the bags under her eyes. What did he expect if she'd been awake most of the night, reaching out for his hand in the bed beside her, or, worse still, scared she was falling in love?

His voice seemed to soften—or was it just her imagination? 'Good morning, Emily.'

Cautiously Emily returned the greeting. 'Marco.' She could see Annie's glance from one to the other and she prayed her daughter would hold her questions till later.

She made an effort to forestall her. 'Dr D'Arvello has been very good when I was worried.'

'*Si*. But today you look worried again.' He smiled at Annie and then back at Emily. She wanted to look away but couldn't because it felt too damn good to bask in the light. 'All is good. Annie's baby has increased the amount of liquid in the uterus quite substantially, which is a good sign of kidney function. I am very pleased.'

Emily felt one burden ease. 'That's wonderful news. So we can go?'

'*Si*. But Annie must rest. I have clinics for another two weeks and I would like Annie to have another ultrasound at the end of this week and see me Friday morning in the rooms here.'

She glanced at Annie, who nodded. 'Fine. We can do that.' That meant one more definite time she would see Marco and the occasional ward sighting. She could handle that. Just.

'So you'll be here for a while?' Annie was on a different track, a mission of her own, and Emily's neck prickled.

'*Si.* I have said I will work and do the on-call before I leave for the States.'

Annie looked so sweet and Emily's trepidation grew. She knew that look. 'So you have no family here, do you?'

Emily froze, wanted to put her hand out or even over her daughter's mouth as she sensed what was coming.

'No.' Marco wasn't stupid either and Emily held her breath.

So innocent Annie. 'Would you like to come to my baby shower?'

'Annie!' Emily's voice came out strangled.

'I'll see.' Marco's smile was crooked. 'Perhaps your mother would prefer if I didn't?'

Annie feigned horror. 'Mum!'

Emily knew she was trapped. 'What?'

Annie cajoled, 'Well, I'd like to invite Rodney and his friends and maybe you could invite Dr D'Arvello and yours?'

Emily's face reddened. 'We'll see. I'm sure Dr D'Arvello has other plans.' She hoped.

Marco didn't offer anything and she glared at him as she was obliged to fill the gap. 'But of course he's welcome.'

Annie was full of mischief. 'You could even come home this afternoon and help us put up the decorations for Mum's birthday.'

Emily blinked in shock. It got worse. 'Annie! That's enough.'

He looked at Emily. 'It is your birthday?'

'Not until Friday.'

Annie sighed. Rolled her eyes. 'Okay. I've already invited Rodney.' She grinned at Marco.

'If you get bored you can get the address from my notes.'

Marco smiled at her. 'Strangely, I know where you live.'

Annie nodded as if he had just confirmed her suspicions. 'I thought you might.' She glanced at her mother's red cheeks.

Going down in the lift Emily fumed. She gripped the handle of Annie's overnight bag and squeezed it until the plastic bit into her fingers. She'd kill her. The little witch had planned that.

She speared a look at her daughter and Annie was innocently staring at the numbers on the console. Avoiding her, as well she should.

Emily stopped grinding her teeth. 'Please don't invite any more people without asking me, Annie.'

Annie swung to face her. Mischief clear and bold. 'Oh, come on. You two can't keep your eyes off each other.' Annie raised her brows and for a moment she looked like her grandmother and Emily felt her anger drain away like water from a leaky pipe.

Until her daughter said, 'And for the record, who was it who said if you like a boy enough to want to have sex, it would be good to let me into the secret?' She grinned cheekily. 'I hope I don't have to discuss contraception with you, Mum.'

It was that obvious? Emily buried the fingers of her free hand into her forehead. This was all too much. She felt like the daughter here. 'Touché.' She huffed her breathe out. 'He is a nice man but he's leaving soon.'

'Come off it, Mum. The guy's gorgeous and he's smitten with you. Even more reason to have some fun, for goodness' sake. And Friday is your birthday.'

Who was this young woman? Then again, Annie had no idea how much fun her mother had already had. Her ears heated. 'I'll think about it.'

By the time she'd driven home and Annie was settled into the big squishy living room chair with her feet up, Emily had calmed down. She even whipped up a batch of date scones to set on the table with butter and jam. Men were always hungry. She couldn't help feeling it would be a bit of an anticlimax if Marco didn't turn up along with Rodney.

She glanced out the window. A black Aston Martin stopped across the road.

Marco turned off the engine. He'd been kidding himself that he wouldn't come. He was glad now because he could see Rodney sitting in his car, staring at the front gate. He'd bet the young man tried to build up the courage to knock on the door.

Marco crossed the street and knocked on Rodney's car roof. 'Hello?'

'Oh. Hi.' Rodney drooped in his seat.

Marco bent down. 'You are coming in?'

Rodney poked his finger down his T-shirt. 'I don't think Annie's mother likes me.'

Marco opened his door. 'Annie's mother will like anyone who makes her daughter happy. You can come with me. We will go in together. Your lady will be glad to see you.'

Marco wasn't real sure about his own lady but he could understand her reluctance to become more involved when he had stated his intention to leave.

Today he was going to help Rodney.

It would be cathartic to help. To help an insecure boy like Marco had been all those years ago. He certainly would have benefited from some advice from another man.

To Emily it must have seemed as if Marco and Rodney had arrived at the same time and she opened the door with a smile that welcomed.

She greeted them both warmly and he couldn't

help his relief. Though why he was surprised was a measure of his own insecurity because she had always been polite.

'Come in. Welcome. Annie will be pleased to see you and we have scones ready.'

The house floated on the aroma of fresh baking, Emily's cheeks were flushed, and Annie lorded over them all from her chair.

It felt like a family. He swallowed the fear in his throat.

Or how he imagined a family would feel. He shouldn't be here. Only when his father had been in jail had he had any idea of a stable life with his mother and he'd been ready to leave home by then. Was there any chance one day his life might come to this?

'Marco, can you help, please?' Perhaps Emily had sensed his ambivalence because she didn't leave him to ponder too deeply for long.

Within minutes industry ensued as Emily directed and he could see where her daughter had inherited her organisational skills from.

A doting Rodney carried buttered scones across to his lady and Marco lifted down the heavy box of decorations that overflowed with a family history he could only imagine. Even at a glance he could tell some of them were very old.

'Thanks.' Emily peered in. 'That's the hardest part—getting that box down from the top of the cupboard.'

She lifted a handful of paper chains from the box, some of them falling apart, and set them on the table ready to hang or repair.

'Annie and I make these every year with the greeting cards from her birthday we saved from the year. So there's lots of them. It's a family tradition. We usually put them up a week before someone's birthday so that they can really soak in the lead-up.'

'A birthday that lasts for a week?' Marco had

very few memories of any celebrations for his
birthday.

Emily looked a little embarrassed. 'It was really for Annie and Gran more than me. Some
of these are from when Annie was only a tod-
dler and just started to play with paper. See, that
strip has part of her fourth birthday card on it.'

Marco shook his head and tried to imagine
a home that stayed still long enough to hoard
such things.

Rodney carried the ladder inside and they discussed their plan of attack.

Emily grinned at him. 'You'll be sorry you
came. By the time you've finished blowing up
the balloons—and they're big ones that Annie
loves—you'll be exhausted. I've been dreading
that job.'

Marco's first sight of the balloons confirmed
the reason she'd dreaded the thought.

'They're huge.' Rodney was wide eyed.

Emily shook her head sadly. 'I know. I had a pump but it broke and I've never got around to buying a new one.'

She frowned at the bag of hand-sized balloons. 'I should insist on the little ones, these ones kill me.' She looked up. 'But Annie loves these.'

'Maybe we could just do a couple?' Rodney was looking dubiously at the balloon in his hand.

'Not this year,' Marco said with finality and a sideways look at Emily. 'In these matters a woman's wish is law. Perhaps if we do them one at a time, we will survive.'

They achieved the impossible, twelve enormous balloons, and all stood around admiringly at the colourful clump on the floor.

'Rodney looks sick.' Annie squinted worriedly at her beau.

'It's just a little headache,' Rodney said gallantly, and Marco patted his shoulder.

'Just.' Emily smiled at Marco and Rodney was

given a kiss by Annie. 'We could not have done that without your big lungs. Thank you, both.'

Rodney blushed and Marco whispered in an aside, 'That is why we do what they want. Worth it?' Rodney nodded carefully.

'So, Annie, if you tell Rodney where to hang the chains, Marco and I will sort the balloons. We'll have it all finished by lunch.'

Much hilarity ensued as every time Rodney stretched the chains the loop broke and they had to strengthen the strips until Marco demanded a stapler and they began to staple the links together.

'Some are older than others and fragile.' Annie defended their chain and Marco shook his head. 'Next birthday perhaps you could start with the stapler and then hang them.' He glanced across and Emily was watching him.

Her face was quietly thoughtful. He saw her acknowledge that he would not be here for the next birthday. Or the one after that, because he had no continuity like these women and their years of family traditions epitomised by this handmade diary of life.

Suddenly he needed fresh air and a cold breeze on his face to snap him out of melancholy. He pulled his phone from his pocket. Pretended to glance at it. 'Excuse me. I need to make a call.'

He left her standing in the middle of the room and Emily watched him go. She couldn't help but wonder about his childhood. What had formed the man who froze at the idea of permanence? She crossed to the kitchen and looked out the window. He wasn't on the phone. He was staring at the empty bird feeder and the silhouette of his face made her ache for the loneliness she saw in his usually smiling face.

She turned, picked up the seeds for the birds, and followed him out. 'The lorikeet isn't here today.'

'I should not have come.'

'Why? Because you don't think you're welcome?'

'Because I cannot have a healthy future with any woman.' He turned to face her squarely. Lifted his head. 'I cannot be the man you deserve, Emily.'

Emerrrlee. Yes, it would have been nice. More than nice to have a normal, evolving relationship with Marco. One with a future and stability and new excitement every day. But in reality life wasn't like that, she of all people knew that, and from this last hour she'd discovered she was still glad she'd connected with Marco D'Arvello and really believed she always would be.

She wished she knew what had him running so scared from forming relationships. 'We don't have to be intensely involved in each other, Marco. The last couple of days were just a mirage for both of us.

'But if you want a family to join for the next couple of weeks before you head off on your next high-powered assignment, please join mine.'

She spread her hands. 'We'd love to have you. Anyone who blows up my balloons is welcome at my door any time.'

He smiled but the humour was missing. 'I worry that it will be difficult for you when I leave.'

Maybe it would be difficult for him too? She shrugged. 'My problem, not yours. I'm single, free to have what friends I choose, and I think regret for time we could have spent together could be worse than being safe with no friendship at all.'

She touched his arm. 'But it's up to you.'

That night at work Emily couldn't help thinking about the day. How it hadn't been as awkward as she'd expected it would be. How Marco had been unobtrusively supportive of Rodney and Annie, and circumspect with her. Maybe too circumspect, according to Annie's view of her mother's love life.

But the idea of just getting to know Marco without actually touching him could be a good idea, could help her see that a globetrotting, super-specialist was not in the realms of reality for her life. The problem was she really did like the caring man she could see beneath the handsome exterior.

Today she'd been glad he'd come back inside. Stayed another hour and helped. Had steadied her while she'd climbed the ladder and precariously placed the last balloon on the lightshade so that everyone clapped when it was done.

The phone rang and she blinked her way back to on-duty. 'Maternity, Emily.'

'Emergency Department. We're sending up a thirty-four-weeker in prem labour. Helen Roberts.

She's a booked Caesarean for foetal abnormality and we have the team coming in for that if you can get her ready. We're up to our ears down here.'

She knew Helen from the antenatal clinic. 'No problem. Thanks.' Emily put the phone down and scooted over to the cupboard with all the pre-admission notes for the women booked to have their babies with Sydney Harbour Hospital.

She pulled Helen's notes and flipped them open on her way back to the desk. 'Prem labour coming in.' Helen would be stressing.

'Must be the month for it.' Lily reappeared from her ward round with a torch.

'Helen was a booked Caesarean for next month. Baby has an oomphaceal picked up on late ultrasound. I'll grab the IV stuff and theatre clothes if you set up the catheter trolley.'

'Who's going to Theatre with them?' Lily was

an experienced plastic surgery nurse and Emily was the more experienced with Caesareans.

'I'll go this time because I know her, and you hold the ward.'

Lily nodded as they hurried together to the sterile storeroom and loaded their trolleys.

Lily was frowning. 'That's a weakness in the skin around the navel, isn't it?'

'Yep. So part of the baby's intestines and sometimes organs are not zipped inside.' Emily grabbed an IV pole with one hand and pushed the trolley with the other. 'The good thing about oomphaceals are the tummy contents are protected by the same membrane that covers the cord. So they're usually safe and can be replaced over time as the skin grows and makes room until it can be replaced inside the abdomen. Or they can have surgery earlier.'

'Imagine the mum.' Lily shook her head. 'It must be hard to be told your baby has something like that. You'd want to see your baby's face in your mind but you'd have to be thinking about his tummy.'

Emily glanced at Lily as they hurried down to an empty room, set up their work areas and turned down the bed. 'That's very true. Helen's amazing, though. I do wonder if sometimes the imagination is much worse than the actual reality.' She grinned. 'You and Luke not getting clucky, are you?'

'Us?' Lily shook her head but she did blush. Emily let it go with a smile. Lily changed the subject. 'I'll bet this mum will be looking forward to seeing her baby. Then she can stop imagining so much.'

They heard the lift doors open and Lily went out to direct them down the hall. Emily leaned over, stuck the name badge to the wall and shifted the bed across so the trolley could come in easily.

She was surprised to see Marco accompany the trolley but he'd said he was on call tonight. Apparently he'd offered to do call for the rest of the week so there'd be no more Limoncello for him when he got home from work.

CHAPTER TEN

HE SMILED at her and it was crazy, but just for that split second she felt the room light up and her heart swell. Then it was gone. She greeted her patient as she arrived at the door.

'Hello, there, Helen. Your baby decided to do this in a rush?'

'Hi, Emily. It started all of a sudden.' Helen looked pale and anxious and Emily touched her hand in sympathy.

She gestured to Helen's belly. 'Maybe she decided it was time she called the shots? Where's Ned?'

Helen grimaced. 'Minding the kids. We couldn't get anyone at such short notice.'

Emily nodded. 'I'll stay with you until he can

get here.' She glanced up at Marco. 'It will take us about ten minutes to get Helen ready. Then I'll come down with her.'

Marco leaned down and smiled at Helen. 'I'll see you in Theatre.' He patted her shoulder and sent one last look Emily's way before he was gone.

Emily glanced at the porter who'd helped Marco push the trolley. 'So you'll come back here for us as soon as you drop the baby resuscitation trolley in Theatre?'

'Okeydoke.' The man smiled at their patient. 'See you in a minute.'

The next seven minutes saw Helen admitted, changed into a gown and hat, and an IV cannula inserted for the fluids she'd need before the epidural anaesthetic.

Emily and Lily worked steadily and Helen breathed quietly through the contractions as they finished each task.

'One thing to go,' Emily said. 'I know we've been attacking you from both sides, but now I have to pop a catheter into your bladder before the surgery. When they reach the uterus, if the bladder isn't completely empty and flat, there's a small risk it could be damaged.'

Helen nodded. 'The sooner it's done, the sooner we go. I read the book you gave me on Caesareans, so I've got a bit of an idea what's happening.'

Emily ticked off the last of the list. 'Lovely. But just ask if you need to.'

Within minutes everything was done. The orderly came back, Emily handed over the keys for the ward to Lily, and they were on their way.

After the epidural was inserted in the anaesthetic bay they pushed Helen through into Theatre and the first person Emily saw inside was Marco—but that may have been because he towered over the others.

He had his head back and was chuckling at something he'd said to the attractive theatre sister. The sight sent an unfamiliar ache through her chest and she glanced back at her patient. 'You okay there?'

When she looked up Marco was by their side and he introduced the man who'd followed their trolley in.

Marco gestured. 'This is our head of paediatrics, Teo Kauri, Helen. Teo's standing by for the arrival of your daughter and he's brought Dr Luke Williams, our plastic surgeon, and a bevy of neonatal nurse specialists so your baby will be in very good hands.'

Helen nodded, a little tearfully, and Marco squeezed her shoulder. Emily thought briefly of Lily back on the ward. Luke and Lily were such a perfect couple, and Luke was introducing himself to Helen with that special smile that Lily raved about.

She was in very good hands, Emily thought to herself, and couldn't help the tiny prayer she sent for her own little granddaughter, who had already benefited from these amazing people. After transfer to the operating table Emily held Helen's hand as the next twenty minutes crept by. Marco gently incised his way down to the uterus, a little more slowly than usual because of the fragile oomphaceal, but still Emily wished it was over. No doubt Helen was a hundred times more impatient than she was.

Emily heard the sound of the suction as the amniotic fluid surrounding baby gushed out, to be captured and removed by the suction tubing. So they'd reached the amniotic sac.

'Not long now.' She squeezed Helen's fingers and watched the neonatal specialists prepare to receive her baby.

The oomphaceal, a greyish-looking balloon on the front of the baby's tummy, wasn't quite as big as Emily had imagined but still it was shocking in weirdness.

Helen's eyes were darting as her imagination tried to make sense of the quiet conversations that were going on. Then Marco's voice. 'Your baby is breathing well and—' He was interrupted by a lusty wail as Helen's baby decided she didn't like being handled by these people.

Everyone laughed with relief and Emily blinked away her own tears. She didn't have a hope of not being affected by the moment. Distantly she heard Marco murmur quietly, 'This is good.'

'Our baby is okay?' Helen was craning her neck. 'Charlotte. We're calling her Charlotte. Charlotte is okay?' Her voice quivered and then the team pushed the neonatal trolley closer and Emily moved out of the way so Mum could reach out and touch her daughter's hand. From the angle she was lying Helen could see the big unfocussed eyes of her daughter as she blinked at the bright lights. The tiny hand closed over her mother's finger and held on tightly.

These were the moments Marco savoured. The naming of a baby. The beginning of a life. Despite the bizarreness of the protruding balloon of organs, this baby would be okay. The mother's fears would be allayed over the coming days, and all would be well.

He saw Emily wipe her eyes and then scoot around the edge of the crowd and snap photos for Helen, and he had to smile at her concentration. But, then, to look at Emily was to smile— and he would do better to put his head down and get on with his work.

But this was a moment he'd always doubted he would ever share with a woman. Many times he had been the outsider but this time he felt closer to the baby than usual. Perhaps it was the fact he had shared the moment with Emily.

Helen's baby was whisked off to the neonatal intensive care unit and Emily and Helen left Theatre an hour later via the NICU. Helen's husband, Ned, arrived just in time to accompany them, and Helen burst into tears with relief.

Teo came across as the trolley was wheeled in. 'Hello, there, again.'

'This is Ned, Charlotte's dad.' Emily introduced the anxious father and Teo shook his hand. Then he bent closer to Helen. 'Congratulations, you two.' He grinned. 'Except for her decision to wear her tummy on the outside, Charlotte looks great.'

They all smiled at that and Helen almost sagged into the bed with relief. Teo went on. 'Because she's four weeks early as well as the tests she needed to undergo, she'll be there for at least a week or two—maybe a little longer if anything crops up. But from our early examinations and tests Charlotte looks good.'

Such a relief. Emily felt her shoulders loosen and she sighed as she smiled. Ned reached down and kissed his wife and Emily turned away to give them some privacy. Such a different birth to experience but so fortunate the team had everything well under control.

'This is good!' Marco had appeared beside her and she looked up at him. This time she didn't care about the tears in her eyes as she shared her joy.

'It's great news.' She turned to Helen's husband. 'Ned, this is Dr D'Arvello. He's the obstetrician who operated on your wife.'

The two men shook hands. 'Thank you, Doctor.'

'My pleasure. It is very rewarding when there is such a good outcome as there is with Charlotte.' He glanced at Emily. Suddenly the impact of not being a part of any family slammed into him. Was he happy with that? Not having what this man in front of him had? What even Emily had with Annie. For ever?

'I will leave you in the very capable hands of the sister and see you later on the ward,' he said, and walked away.

The night passed swiftly after that. Marco came back briefly to check to see his patient was settled and comfortable and to impart the information that despite Charlotte's IV running well she was sucking happily on her fist.

Emily glanced at the clock and wondered again at how he managed with such a full schedule. She'd just happened to look for his next theatre list and saw it commenced in six hours. She left him to his conversation and went back to the desk to clear up the paperwork involved with the birth and there was a mountain of forms to keep her mind occupied.

She didn't hear him approach and Marco took

a moment to just soak her in. Her cap of hair was across her face, her shoulders bent over her work, and he could see the curve of her neck that continued to entrance him. His obsession was becoming troublesome.

She brushed back her hair and held it away with her hand and he could see the frown across her forehead. 'You look worried. Anything I can help with?'

Emily jumped. Looked up and tried not to let him completely destroy her concentration. 'You could go to bed.'

He opened his mouth to say the obvious thing, smiled instead, and they both knew what he'd been going to say.

'Well stopped,' Emily said primly.

'But still thought of.' His smile melted any resistance to loss of concentration. She was a basket case.

'Goodnight, Emily.' He turned and walked

away and she watched his broad back disappear up the corridor.

She sighed.

'What was that sigh for?' Lily plonked the torch up on the shelf after another ward round.

'Nothing.' Emily changed the subject. 'Luke was in Theatre with Marco.'

'Yep. He's on call. I try to do nights when he's on call because most of the time he does come in and that means we can have the days off together. But you changed the subject. Were you sighing after the gorgeous Dr D'Arvello?'

Lily glanced up the hallway as the lift swallowed Marco. A hint of concern in her friend's voice. 'He's going soon, isn't he?'

Like she needed to be reminded of that. Lily cared and was always discreet. Maybe it would help to tell someone. 'I'll stay sensible but I can't help wishing he'd open up a little. Why is it so hard for men to talk about themselves?' She glanced at Lily and smiled ruefully. 'I'm pretty happy to chat about myself if someone asks.'

'Women are used to connecting with people. But he's not different. Luke was like a clam.' She tilted her head and studied Emily's face. 'You really like him, don't you?'

'I don't have any illusions. He'll be gone by the end of the month, but Annie likes him as well. But, then, he did do a lifesaving operation on my grandchild.'

'Always a good reason to like someone.' They both grinned. 'But I think it's more than that. You look at him like I look at Luke. Or Evie looks at Finn. That worried, "are you okay, I care," look that women get when they've chosen their mate.'

'No, I don't.' She stared at her friend. 'I hope I don't. Do I? Lily?'

Lily laughed at the lack of choice people had when they met their match. 'Yeah. I can see you're trying to keep your head free but that must be hard when your daughter invites him to put up decorations and come to her baby shower.'

Emily put her head in her hands. 'It was probably too late anyway.'

Lily's eyes opened wide. 'You've slept with him!'

Emily sighed. 'I could tell you but then I'd have to kill you.'

'Oh.' Lily hugged her. 'He's a very cool guy.'

Emily nodded. Ridiculously proud of him. 'He's amazing. But he has issues. In fact, I have issues. Like he's leaving in a couple of weeks and the more I see of him the harder it's going to be when he leaves. I should stop now.'

Lily laughed and stood up. 'If only it was that easy. And they all have issues. Look at Finn.'

They looked at each other and shook their heads. 'Wouldn't be Evie for quids.'

CHAPTER ELEVEN

EVIE wouldn't have agreed. It wasn't easy but she'd chosen her man and she would make it work. She'd tracked Finn to his office again and this time she shut the door behind her when she went in.

He'd been working on some papers and his eyebrows lifted mockingly. 'Come to take advantage of my previous weakness?'

She was over him pretending they didn't have a mutual attraction. 'I've decided to stake my claim.'

'Claim on what?' He glanced down at himself. 'A broken-down quack with a penchant for princesses?'

She so didn't see him like that. 'I think you're

the most amazing surgeon I've ever met.' She gave him a hard stare. 'And I'm trying to keep you away from barmaids.'

He shook his head. 'I never slept with her, Evie.'

He hadn't? So all that angst had been for nothing. She could feel her temper rise. 'Well, thanks for putting me out of my misery.'

He stood up. Stared at her and then crossed the floor. She held her ground despite the unnerving stare he kept her pinned with. 'Misery is my middle name. You wanna play with me then get used to it.'

'Well, Pollyanna is mine so expect some disagreements.'

He laughed, short and sharp, and to her relief his face softened. 'Why on earth would a gorgeous girl like you want me? How long do you seriously think this is going to last?'

'I was hoping for ever.'

He pulled her in and held her against him and she knew this was where she wanted to be. She knew how hard it must have been for him to make the decision to let her into his very private world and she still couldn't believe her luck. She hugged him and even the tiny easing of his tension made her feel hopeful.

'I love you, Finn.'

This time he crushed her against his chest but it was over too soon. She tried not to be disappointed he couldn't bring himself to return the declaration.

Her whole damn childhood had been like that. Cold emotions, brick walls between her parents—she didn't want that with Finn. Surely she hadn't chosen a man that would freeze her out like her father had frozen her mother out?

But she wasn't as easily bowed as her mother. She'd make him join the human race if it killed her. Or him.

'A little bit of feedback wouldn't go astray here, Finn.'

Finn strangled back a laugh. Not a sound she heard nearly enough but it was so good to hear it now. 'Evie, you are some woman.'

'I know. It's about time you appreciated me.' She needed to hear this.

His hard blue eyes softened further. 'Oh, I do. Don't you worry.'

Like blood from a stone. 'I repeat. Some feedback would be good.'

'I didn't realise you were so needy.' The old Finn was back.

Ohh. She could strangle him. 'You don't realise much at all do you, Finn, that isn't directly related to Sydney Harbour Hospital? You live and breathe this place and I'm asking that you cut yourself a little slack to think about the outside world.'

'Why?' He shot her hard look. 'Because you

think I might have to give it up? Is that it, Evie? Is this another discussion leading to that experimental surgery?' As if he was surprised she'd brought it up again.

Well, yes. 'If I don't have that discussion with you, who will?' She pointed her finger at him. 'You'll shut down any of your few friends that dare to bring it up.'

He shrugged and turned away.

'You'll block out your doctor's recommendations.'

Finn laughed again but this time Evie didn't like the sound. 'It's been done before. Happens to me with my patients all the time.'

She wasn't listening to excuses. 'I might be your only chance, Finn. And I'm going to push until you face the reality. There is no choice.'

'There is a choice, Evie!' He turned and faced her and this time she saw, way at the back of his eyes, the fear of being less than a man. 'At least if I don't have the operation I can walk away. If I have it I might be flat on my back without that choice.'

She stepped up to him. Wrapped her arms around him and he stood stiff in her embrace. 'You can't put up with this pain for ever, Finn.'

Still he wouldn't lean into her. 'I'm putting up with it now.'

She stepped back so she could see his face. Plead her case. 'You're drinking too much. Your analgesia is becoming ineffective, the exercise that used to help isn't doing its job any more.'

He glared at her. Building barriers faster than she could break them down. 'If you can't stand the way I am then get out, Evie.'

She shook her head. Glared right back. 'You'd like that, wouldn't you? That way you could just go back to drowning out life along with the pain and self-destruct in your own time.'

He didn't deny it.

'Well.' She put her hands on her hips. 'I reiterate, I love you, Finn Kennedy, and I'm going to fight tooth and nail for you and the life we could have together. It's your job to make that decision.'

Still no response. She took a deep breath and dived in where very few had dared. 'You need to take the step to stop suffering physically and emotionally from the explosion that killed your brother, Finn.'

His eyes blazed. 'That's enough.'

She nodded. Not surprised, and sorry she'd had to hurt him, but he needed to break through the barrier. 'It probably is.'

She stepped away. Physically and mentally. 'I'm too frustrated to talk to you any more today, Finn.'

Finn watched her go. Damn her. Well, he wasn't chasing her every time she got the huffs.

* * *

By Wednesday Finn was looking for Evie. He'd had three horrendous nights' sleep, the pain was getting worse and he'd dropped his keys beside his car this morning and they'd almost gone down a manhole. Maybe he did need to consider the op.

Now, for the first time in his life, he wanted to share his thoughts with another person. Apparently that was what she wanted, but Evie was giving him the cold shoulder, and now he couldn't find her. Maybe he'd driven her away with his disgusting temper but he'd thought she had more staying power than that.

'There you are.' She was suturing a boy's hand in the emergency room theatre and she looked amazing. He felt like hell.

'I've been here on and off for the last three days, Finn. What can I do for you?'

Well, she couldn't do much for him while she had that laceration to fix. 'Lunch. At one. At

Pete's. Talk about that thing we talked about. That suit you?'

Evie didn't smile but he had the suspicion she was having trouble keeping it in. That made him smile. 'Don't be late.'

Emily, Evie and Lily finally made it to coffee.

Emily invited them all to the baby shower and then stopped and reached across and squeezed Evie's hand. 'So how is Finn?'

'I can tell you girls because I know you don't gossip.' Evie lifted her head and they could see she was okay. Emily was glad. 'Cranky as a cut snake but I actually think I'm finally getting through.'

Lily grinned. 'If anyone can—you can!'

Evie smiled. 'Early days yet, but I'm quietly confident. How are you and Luke going, Lily?'

Lily's face lit up and there really wasn't a need for her words. 'I'm in seventh heaven.'

They both looked at Emily. 'And what about you and Marco?'

'It's complicated.'

'It always is.'

Emily sighed. 'I'm just going with the flow but I'm scared of getting too close. It's not long till he leaves.'

Evie nodded. 'At least he's here for your birthday on Friday.'

Emily sighed again. 'Annie's been onto you. And I don't even know if he'll come.'

Lily grinned. 'We discussed it while she was in hospital and of course he'll come.'

'I hope nobody spends money on me!'

Lily shook her head. 'I know you hate that. Just friends for tea. I told Annie I didn't think it was a good idea to surprise someone who's just come off nights. So she knows I was going to tell you.'

'Finn's coming.' The other two girls looked at Evie.

'No wonder you're quietly confident,' Lily said.

The next two days flew by. Emily didn't see Marco as the theatres were particularly busy, and she knew she would see him on Friday for Annie's appointment.

Then there was the looming non-surprise party but she couldn't worry about that. She had no doubt that Lily and Evie would have her best interests at heart even if it was the last thing she wanted. Inside a little voice whispered plaintively and wondered if Marco would come.

Emily's birthday started on Friday with a busy shift in the early hours and Annie's post-ultrasound appointment was scheduled before Emily could have her after-work sleep.

Happy birthday just didn't seem the same when you wanted your bed.

So when Marco and Annie decided to talk about her, not to her, during the appointment, Emily's sense of humour was far from tickled.

Annie lay on the examination couch as Marco palpated her abdomen. Ah, Marco thought. Even abdominally they could tell Annie's baby was growing. 'So this baby of yours is feeling better. See the height of your belly has come up to here, that is more than a centimetre.'

'That's what the ultrasonographer said. It's great.' Annie sat up. 'So when are you taking my mother out?'

Marco helped her step down and studiously avoided looking at Emily. 'Do you think I should?'

Annie tilted her head and for a moment she looked older than her sixteen years. 'How many more days do you have to waste?'

She was correct. Marco could not resist a glance across the room. Emily had turned and walked over to the window to look out over the harbour. A delightful pink tide had risen to her ears. He had always admired that soft curve of her neck. He lowered his voice. 'Not many. But perhaps your mother has seen enough of me.'

He saw Annie glance at her mother's back. Mischief danced in those green eyes so like Emily's. 'She likes you.' She shrugged and grinned at him. 'I like you. And she doesn't have much fun. She seems to think that apart from work she's bad if she's away from me.'

'That's enough, you two. I'm not some charity that needs supporting.' She glared at her daughter then at Marco, and he had to smile at the fire in her eyes. He knew she was a passionate woman. He'd seen what she could do to butter with a knife.

'I think your mother needs to rest so she can enjoy her day. We are *finito* here. Your baby is doing as well as I hoped.'

'Will we see you tonight at Mum's party?' It seemed nothing would suppress Annie's intention to meddle.

'I have a very long theatre list but as soon as it is over it would be my pleasure to come.' He looked across at Emily. 'Is this fine with you?

Emily sighed and nodded. Her weary smile reminded him of the day of Annie's surgery and how he'd wished then to tuck her into a feather bed. And that had been before Emily had shown him a world he hadn't believed existed. His heart squeezed painfully in his chest as he acknowledged he'd become drawn into the magic world of the Cooper women. It would be hard to leave.

'Of course.' She crossed the room and held out her hand like she had the first day he'd met her. He took it and lifted it to his lips. *'Buon compleanno.* Happy birthday, Emily.'

Emily slept surprisingly well—perhaps because of the news Annie's baby was better, or maybe because of the truce between her and Marco. Or the fact she would see him tonight.

When she woke Lily and Annie and Rodney had quietly done all the work and she could just sit back and enjoy.

Emily's party was a huge success. Pete's Bar had catered and he'd outdone himself with mini beef pies and brilliant entrées that melted in the mouth and kept coming so that the little alcohol imbibed was soaked up nearly as fast as it went down.

Annie's portable music system belted out songs everyone knew and a few of Annie's strange modern ones she couldn't resist, though Rodney kept a firm eye on the content in honour of Emily's advancing age and delicate sensibilities.

The girls, unbeknownst to Emily, had requested gifts but set with a price limit to two dollars. That guaranteed some hilarious choices.

The paediatrican, Teo, had declared himself

fairy godfather and handed out the gift-wrapped surprises one by one to Emily. There was something about a wide and mischievious Polynesian grin and a man with a pink wand that made everyone smile.

His new wife, Zoe, kept slipping up for a sit on the fairy godfather's knee whenever there was a vacancy and Emily shared the envious glances from other single women at the blatant happiness that shone from Zoe's face.

Finn was there, not scowling quite as hard as usual, and when Evie handed their gift to Emily, a flashing faux bejewelled tiara, she looked more relaxed than she had for a while.

Lily and Luke were cuddled up in the corner discreetly, chuckling over the pair of his-and-hers shower caps they'd given Emily, and Annie and Rodney had splashed out on a weather vane for the back yard that they thought Emily would laugh at.

Emily smiled and thanked everyone and had a good time, but she couldn't help wonder if Marco would manage to slip across for half an hour before it all ended. Teo had said he'd finished his operating list late but at least it was finished. Not that she should be getting in any deeper with a man who was leaving but it was so hard not to look forward to just seeing him. Even feeling his presence and basking a little in the unmistakable pleasure he seemed to have in her company was worth it.

Someone touched her on the shoulder and as she turned slowly she knew even from that light caress whose hand it was. She couldn't help the pleasure that welled. 'Well, hello, there. You made it.'

His eyes crinkled as he smiled down at her. 'I heard there was a particularly delightful princess coming tonight.'

He tweaked the silver crown Emily had forgotten she wore and she grinned up at him. 'All the best princesses wear jewels like this.'

'And *buon compleannao.* Happy birthday, again, beautiful Emily.' He handed her his present.

She felt the package with her eyes shut then opened them still mystified. 'You know it can't be worth more than two dollars?'

He grinned. 'Of course.'

She undid the wrapping and then she smiled with a wobble of her lip because suddenly she wanted to cry. 'It's beautiful.' She looked up at him mistily. 'Thank you.'

'Let me see!' Annie had dragged Rodney across to welcome Marco and she looked down at the little pink mouse with wheels. 'Huh? So what does it do?'

Marco took the mouse from Emily and wound the key. Then he bent down and pointed it towards the wall. It zipped along in erratic directions until finally it hit the skirting board. Emily got the giggles and her daughter looked at her.

Annie tugged Rodney's hand to go back to the music. 'That's a weird present,' Emily heard her say, and the giggles came back.

Marco watched her indulgently. 'Did you sleep today after Annie's appointment?'

'Of course. My usual four hours. It's been a big week for you, too.'

'Unlike you, I at least go back to my bed at night. Do you still have to do this night shift? Your daughter is old enough now to not need you to work such abnormal hours.'

She shrugged. 'It's what I do. One day I will stop but someone has to pay the bills.'

Marco frowned. He could understand that. And it was none of his business. He needed to remember that. In fact, he was mad even turning up here, but he did hate it that Emily was as tired as she'd looked that morning. Had worried about her all day at the back of his mind during his surgery list.

For the last few years his financial concerns had improved so much they'd been delegated to a financial planner. A very good one. Never again would he worry where his next meal came from, or even his next house should he wish to purchase one, but he didn't like the idea that Emily had such concerns.

Emily frowned at him and he realised he'd overstepped the boundaries of their relationship. Again. He didn't even know why he'd started that conversation and she had every right to look at him strangely. He changed topic abruptly. 'I was pleased with Annie's ultrasound today.'

'She's happy. She asked when you were coming over again for a barbecue.'

'Is that an invitation?' He had become so needy it sickened him.

'You know you're welcome any time.'

But would he see her alone? He had his other gift to give. Annie he enjoyed, she made him smile, but it seemed like a year since he'd had Emily to himself. 'It's a shame I can't run you home after the party.'

She smiled and in her beautiful eyes he saw the acknowledgement that she too missed their time together but accepted the reality of no future. 'That would be hard when I live here.'

'I could drive you around the block. Then drop you home.' It seemed his heart was not yet ready to listen to reason.

'Or you could just stay back when everyone goes.' Perhaps her heart wasn't ready, either. She tilted her head. 'But I don't know if night-time is a good time to be alone with you, Marco.'

Now he could not give in. 'It could be a very good time.'

'That's what I mean.' Wistful perhaps. He hoped.

'Afraid?' Always a trump card with Emily. The dare.

'Of you?' She arched her brows. 'Not likely. I've been stuck to a wall upside down in a ride with you.'

He laughed. Could feel the lightness of heart that he had come to realise was how he felt whenever he was with Emily. 'So may I stay?'

She glanced around. Everyone was starting to leave. The party was almost over and what mischief could they get into when Annie was here? What harm could be done with sharing his company just a little longer? 'Of course. But you can explain to Annie. I'll just say goodbye to people. Do you want to come?'

Not really. Was it wise to advertise the fact they were together? Perhaps he needed to get over this aversion to being paired with one woman. Paired with Emily. He had never worried about parading a beautiful woman on his arm before. He would be gone and forgotten in another couple of weeks. So why was this different?

'As you wish.' There must have been the remains of his discomfort in his voice because she swivelled back to face him.

'Is there a problem?'

'No.' He thought about it. Tasted his reasoning. Fear? Fear of what? 'No, there isn't. I'm sorry. Let us say goodbye together.'

She looked at him strangely, as well she might, but he'd had an epiphany. He realised he was proud to be seen with Emily. Even if it was for a few short weeks he would carry the memories with him for a long time and he was far from ashamed that she enjoyed his company.

He held out his hand and smiled at her. 'Come.'

She took his hand. Grinned at his word choice. 'It's just Evie and Finn and Lily and Luke mostly. They organised this with Annie.'

When he shook hands Finn grinned and Marco acknowledged the satire behind the smile. Evie hugged him but he was not sure why and Luke and Lily smiled warmly when Emily said Marco was staying for a while.

Maybe it wasn't so bad to face the world with someone you were proud of. He realised he was proud of Emily. Proud of the amazing woman she was. He just hoped she felt the same. But he would like at least a few moments alone with her.

'Would you like to go for a walk?'

'With a big strong man as my escort? Why not? I don't usually walk around here at night on my own.'

The thought sent a shiver of disquiet through him. Emily alone at night. 'I should hope not.'

Emily heard the possessiveness in his voice. Couldn't help but smile at it. A woman could get used to a man who wished to ensure her safety.

Wanted to protect her. A woman could—but Emily wouldn't have that opportunity. Marco would be gone and she would be travelling alone again shortly. 'I could walk at night if wanted to.'

He laughed. 'And if you had a butterknife, any man would be afraid.'

She called out to Annie to say they'd be down at the wharf and they walked out into the street together.

They walked with purpose, hand in hand, neither quite relaxed enough to dawdle—perhaps the idea of time marching on kept their pace fast, as if they could squeeze as much distance covered into the short time they had together.

The sensation of walking with Marco by her side seemed bitter-sweet for Emily until they came to the pier where the ferries came in.

He reached into his pocket for the gift box that had arrived by courier from the airport. More notice of her birthday would have been good. 'I have something else for your birthday. Something from Italy to remember me by.'

It didn't sound as good as he'd hoped when he said it like that.

She took the box hesitantly and he shook his head. 'I do not buy much. It will give me pleasure to give you this.'

She nodded, smiled up at him, and he savoured her reluctance to tear the paper. Finally it was open and the brilliantly hued heart-shaped pendant shimmered in the streetlight. Such brilliant greens that matched her eyes. Exactly as he'd wished.

'It is Murano crystal. Made in Venice.' He took it from her and indicated he would help her fasten it. 'May I?'

'Of course.' She turned and exposed her nape and his stupid fingers shook as he fastened it.

'It's beautiful. Thank you.' She leant up and kissed his cheek. 'I will treasure it.'

And I will treasure the memories of you, she thought, and turned away to hide her face from him.

She pointed out the big old house on the water. 'So my little house is tucked in behind there.'

Marco stared thoughtfully at the huge white mansion. 'And that was your grandfather's childhood home?'

'Yes.' They both looked at the untidy lawn that ran down to the water's edge. 'But it was sold well before he met Gran to pay his father's debts.'

A ferry glided in, churned the water, and reversed away again as they leant on the rail and gazed over Sydney harbour.

There was a certain melancholy in their comfortable silence. 'Would you like to catch the next ferry to Luna Park for an hour?'

She smiled and shook her head. 'I have my mouse now.'

He lifted her hand to his mouth and kissed her palm. The movement drew her towards him and she stepped in closer. By the light of the streetlamp his chiselled features stood out starkly and she lifted her other hand to stroke his cheek. 'Thank you for coming to my party.'

'I needed to see those decorations in all their glory.' She was going to joke back when he broke in again.

'Already I miss you, Emily.'

Her brows drew together and she looked across at him. 'We must be sensible.' And then he kissed her and neither felt very sensible at all as he pulled her into the shadows away from the pool of yellow light cast by the streetlamp.

Marco's mouth trailed her throat and she slipped her fingers in between the buttons of his shirt. Splayed them across his chest because who knew if she would ever feel this chest again? The warmth of reality, so firm and strong beneath her palm. She turned her head so she could hear his heart beat like a drum against her ear. Then his mouth came down again and he lifted her, spun her in the way she loved, and she wrapped her arms around his shoulders as she stared down into his face. A face she saw so often now in her dreams. A face that would soon be gone, and the added fuel of that thought deepened her response as she lost herself in his embrace.

Rodney's running footsteps penetrated and Marco lowered her until her feet touched down as the kiss broke. His arm steadied them as they turned.

'Here you are!' The relief on Rodney's face sent a shiver of alarm through Emily's whole body. 'You have to come home. She's got pains.'

Emily could feel the fear balloon in her chest. She should have noticed something was wrong. And she hadn't been there. She'd been out kissing Marco in the shadows. What sort of mother was she?

The three of them jogged up the hill until they reached the house and then Marco followed more slowly. This was not good. 'What time did the pains start?' he asked Rodney.

'Just after you left. But she didn't tell me till just now. I was going to ring Emily but she wouldn't let me.'

Stupido. 'Afraid of the false alarm. Next time you tell her she must. Do not take no.'

Rodney nodded but he looked alarmed that he might have done the wrong thing. Marco patted his shoulder. 'It is good you are here and that you came for us. Wait. I will see what is happening.'

Before he could make his way to Annie's room Emily was back. 'Her waters have broken. She's in full labour.'

So. As he'd feared. 'Take your car. It will be faster than an ambulance and we both have the experience. I will phone ahead and they will meet us with a trolley.'

Emily's eyes were anguished and he wanted to pull her in close and comfort her. But there would be time later.

'What if the baby comes?'

He squeezed her shoulder. 'Then we will manage. It is our work. We are minutes from the hospital. Get the car and I will carry her out.'

Emily couldn't remember the drive. Just that this was real and it was happening. And she hadn't been there. Rodney held Annie's hand and Emily tried desperately to pretend her daughter was a woman she didn't know. Her voice was calm, steady, matter-of-fact when Annie started to panic, was this transition stage already, and deep inside Emily wanted to scream and beat her chest and say *'No!* I'm sorry.'

They arrived in the ambulance bay within minutes and, thanks to Marco's call, were transported immediately to the birthing suite where others were already assembled.

Teo was there, and his team from the NICU was there, even one who had been here when Annie herself had been born.

And always Marco. Calm, organised, directing the administration of drugs, acknowledging there was little they could do to halt the birth of Annie's baby but secure in the knowledge the best of neonatal care was waiting.

Twenty-seven weeks. Thirteen weeks early. Emily was transported back through the years to the day her own baby had been born. To the strangeness of the NICU, to the fragility of her own newborn. But that would be nothing to what Annie would go through.

Her granddaughter would be tiny. Like a doll in a man's palm, wrinkled and skinny and bright pink with blood too close to the surface through too few layers of skin. Little eyes barely able to open. Too tiny to fight any infection, would forget to breathe, struggle to eat. It would go on for months. And always the risk she would get sick and not see the next day.

Why? Why had this happened? How could she have prevented it? She should never have left the house with Marco.

Marco saw the fears cross Emily's face. Wave after wave. Battered but never beaten. He wanted to stride across the room and shelter her. Calm her storm of fears, but he couldn't. Tell her it would be all right but he wasn't so sure it would.

In his mind he reassured himself. She was strong, she didn't need him. Not someone who would be leaving before this whole drama had played out.

All he knew was this baby was coming. Then Annie's baby arrived.

The next hour was fraught as Rosebud fought for life.

They all moved down to the NICU. Annie, shaking with the hormones of labour, in a wheel-chair, Rodney holding her hand, his eyes red from emotion, Emily hovering, explaining, sup-porting... And Marco...stood apart.

Teo orchestrated the recovery of a perilously ill neonate with his team of intensivists. Men and women who worked like clockwork, a day in their lives pretty much like another, but not for the Cooper family.

Check tube, intubation, the sound of mechanical lungs breathing such minimal breaths for tiny lungs. Rhythmic, relentless, a breath even if she didn't want to. IV lines in veins like patterns drawn by ballpoint, incredibly thin and fragile vessels captured and taped. Skin dots attached to cardiac monitors. Murmured voices discussing the life of your child in equations and gradients and percentages of oxygen for the very prem.

Marco had seen it all many times before. Had

done his time in NICU as a registrar, had chosen the maternal side of birth in preference to this very prem duelling dance with death. Standing there, he knew why.

For Emily, as she eased back away from the open crib until her spine was against the cold nursery wall, suddenly she felt disconnected. Unable to believe this was happening.

It took her back sixteen years. Even though Annie had never been as fragile as this baby, the feelings were the same.

Fear, helplessness and such a sense of loss for the beautiful, tranquil birth and introduction her tiny granddaughter should have had if she'd stayed where she should have.

She sucked in another breath. But she would stay strong for Annie, strong for little Rosebud, even strong for Rodney, who had surprised her with his caring, his inability to hide how much he adored Annie and looked up to her, and his absolute devotion to his tiny daughter.

She wiped a disobedient tear away. She wasn't going to cry. Not here. Not now.

God, she was so sick of being strong.

Sixteen years ago she'd stood against her parents and their wish that she should have her baby adopted, had refused their attempt to sweep her pregnancy and their granddaughter under the mat of public scrutiny.

Her parents had come once to see Annie after the birth, and had refused to even hold her, and that had been when Emily had decided her daughter wouldn't grow up in such a house of disapproval.

On discharge from hospital she'd packed her school things, the few pieces of baby clothes she'd managed to collect and headed to Gran's, where she had been welcomed with open arms.

Emily had been determined, had begun to plan

the future for her daughter and herself, but still inside she'd needed to prove to everyone that she was not just a good mother but the best mother anywhere.

Now she needed to be strong again. She saw Marco watching her. Saw his concern, and for a moment she was tempted to ask for help, pass some of her load across to those broad shoulders, but what if she did? What if she weakened and then suddenly he was gone? What would she do then?

What if having to deal with Marco's departure eroded the well of strength she'd always relied on? She didn't go to anyone when she struggled with life. She just got on with it. The thought terrified her. Soon he'd be gone. If she took strength from him she'd have to start being alone all over again.

And she didn't have the emotional fortitude to spare. Annie and Rosebud needed her. She wouldn't let them down again. It was better she carried the load alone, like she would have to when Marco was gone.

This was family pain of a different sort. Marco watched from across the room.

He ached for Annie, for her tiny baby and especially for Emily, but he could not become involved. Could not cross the floor to stand by her side, no matter how much he wanted to.

She needed someone strong, someone who would always be there for her. He glanced around the room and still she stood alone.

But who would that be?

Such isolation. Suddenly he saw that she was like him. Alone. Isolated. Yet she had not let it affect her ability to welcome people into her circle of caring, like she had admitted him. She made friends, stood by them, opened herself to risk. This he could not do, had never learned, but maybe, one day slowly, he could absorb the rudiments he'd learned from Emily. If he crossed the room, what could he do? He felt so helpless.

Did she blame him? Could he have foreseen Annie would go into prem labour? What if he had kept her in hospital longer? But he knew any other hospital would have done the same. And the speed that she'd laboured would never have been successfully stopped. He had to go to her.

'Emily?' He touched Emily's shoulder. Brushed the hair back from her eyes. 'It is good Rosebud had already had her hydrocortisone and this will stand the lungs in good stead.'

She looked at him but he wasn't sure she could see him. 'I know. But still she's so fragile.'

His hand fell and then he lifted it again. He'd pushed through his fear of becoming too involved with this family. She would not push him away now. 'What can I do? How can I help you?'

She looked at him. Stepped back a pace out of range of his hand. 'I'm fine. We'll get through this. It's what we do. It's what I do. I'm sorry, Marco. I need space. I need to be here for my daughter. For Rosebud.'

No. He could not accept that. Finally a moment that was not about him or his past. This was about Emily, who needed to take his help. He would fight to help her; for the first time in his life he would fight for a woman, he would find a way.

She thought she did not need him. But she did. 'Let me be here for you. Be here for Annie and for her Rosebud. I can be a shoulder to lean on. Perhaps you should learn to share the load.'

'With who, Marco? With you? A man who has already turned my life upside down. Already made me yearn for things I can't have. What we had was good. But it's finished. I don't have time for me right now.' She glanced at her granddaughter. 'Look at her. She's as fragile as a butterfly on her little open cot.' She shook her head. 'I don't have time for you.'

Appropriate for a man passing though. The pain sliced through him like it had in the lift when she'd stepped away from him. Perhaps he should get used to that pain. There was a greater one coming when he flew from Sydney. Marco nodded. He wasn't sure he was finished, but at this moment he wasn't helping. So he walked away.

What did he expect? The doubts eased in as the distance between he and Emily grew. Why should someone want and need him? Nobody ever had. Except for his work. Always he had his work. So back to work and then he would finish here before he caused himself, or Emily, more pain.

But it was much harder than he expected to

walk away from the Coopers. Even more reason to run. He passed Finn and Evie as they came in but he didn't stop.

CHAPTER TWELVE

'I HOPE Emily's granddaughter is okay.' Evie and Finn stood outside the door to Finn's penthouse after visiting the Coopers in the NICU. This was the first time Evie had been back to his flat because they'd both been absolutely snowed under with work—and to be honest she was a little nervous.

'Born on her grandmother's birthday. So I guess if she has as much guts as Emily, she'll make it.'

Finn opened the door and gestured for Evie to precede him. She couldn't help a sliding glance at the wall in his apartment she'd become very acquainted with the last time she was here.

Finn saw the pink in her cheeks and raised his

eyebrows mockingly. She walked swiftly across the room and perched on the edge of the leather lounge. 'I think that's the nicest thing I've ever heard you say, Finn. You sound almost human.'

'Hmph.' He shut the door with a click. She re-membered that from last time too. Goose-bumps feathered along her arms. 'Don't tell anybody.' He crooked his finger. 'Come here.'

She raised her own brows. 'You come here.' Actually, she didn't think her legs would carry her with the way he was looking at her now.

'Okay.' He was across the room in three longs strides and his hand came down and captured hers. He guided her up until she stood hard against his body. 'Let's not talk.'

He was so solid against her. She'd never get used to being this close to Finn. She never wanted to stop being this close to Finn. But she needed to know his decision. 'You said you had something to tell me.'

'In a minute.' His finger lifted her chin and slowly his face came down. 'I need something first.' His mouth took hers with an aching need that grew more searching, more demanding of her strength, exposed her aching love for this embittered man, tried her by the fire of his fears and her own, and the finality of his decision brought tears to her eyes.

He stepped back but she followed him. Thrust her hips against him to anchor him. 'Tell me what you've decided about the operation.'

'It's booked for next Monday.'

The words fell into the quiet room like drips of water in a cave, yet the impact was a ripple of emotion she didn't know how to ride.

She shivered and for a moment she wanted him to change his mind. Not risk the worst-case scenarios of mobility loss or even death. But the alternative was never going to be an option. His pain would continue to spiral upwards as the shrapnel buried deeper, the motor loss in his hands and arms would grow more unpredictable, and the medications would become more useless.

Her arms crept around his waist. 'Then we should make the most of the time we have.'

Finn looked down at her and imperceptibly his face softened. 'Always to the point, Dr Lockheart.'

'The point is, Dr Kennedy, I love you and always will.'

'Always?' Mockingly again but there was a thread of uncertainty in Finn's voice that brought the tears to her eyes.

'It's terminal.'

'Thanks for bringing that up.'

'For God's sake, Finn. Take me to bed.'

He laughed, threaded his fingers through hers, and drew her through to his room.

* * *

A week later the NICU was quiet when Emily called in on the Friday morning after her shift. The lights were dim and it seemed more peaceful than usual. 'All the babies must be behaving,' Emily murmured to herself.

It had been a slow couple of nights and sometimes she wished for the craziness of a busy ward that made the wee small hours fly and the sun come up before she knew it was on its way. Especially when she wanted to divert her mind from drifting to a tall, dark Italian who made her toes curl for what might have been.

Her eyes ached with tiredness, that was all, and the dull headache was because it was nearly time for bed and she hadn't been sleeping as well as she usually did. It was probably all the worry of Rosebud.

She was getting used to her name.

There was an empty chair beside her crib and Emily sank down into it. When she put her chin on her hand she could just sit and soak in the regular in and out of little lungs growing stronger every day. So tiny. So amazingly tough.

She realised that her granddaughter was growing and unfurling like a little blossom. A bud. A rosebud? Emily smiled. Okay. She liked the name.

She looked sturdier, less translucent, and while Emily sat there Rosebud's little arms flexed and her eyelids flickered.

'Hello there, little one.' Emily said softly, and held her breath as Rosebud turned her head and opened her eyes. Emily bit her lip. 'Hello.' Such a tiny little pixie face yet so like her mother's. The little eyelids fluttered and then shut again and Emily sighed back into the chair. 'Wow. Thank you.'

Marco watched Emily from the corner of the room. He carried the coffee he'd taken to drinking with his *piccola rosa*, his little rose, before he started his day. He enjoyed the few moments with his tiny friend but was always careful to be absent when her grandmother was due.

He did not wish to cause Emily pain, though often he stayed, as now, just to catch a glimpse.

He saw her smile from across the room and it pierced his heart. He did not know how much more of this he could stand.

He'd added cases every day to the end of his list so that he could shorten the time he was in Sydney. Perhaps he had done enough. He would look for flights tonight.

Something made Emily glance across the room. Marco stood silently in the corner. How long had he been there? She really didn't think she could do this right now. Every day she had to remind herself he was leaving. Less than a week now.

Perhaps by then this aching wound he'd left in her life would have begun to heal but she was afraid that it hadn't yet ripped all the way to the bone like it would when he flew out.

Now he knew she'd seen him. He was walking towards her. Tall and solemn he still filled her with that fluttery awareness, the intrinsic magnetism she could barely hold out against, and her heart begged her to reach out and touch him.

Emily tucked her hands into her lap. 'I didn't expect to see you here.'

He inclined his head and spoke quietly so as not to startle their baby. 'I visit Rosebud when I can. We are old friends.'

So he came when he was sure he would not run into her. Well, that was what she'd asked for. Unfortunately she could imagine the early mornings or late evenings with Marco and Rosebud in the quiet nursery, communing in the semidarkness, and she felt the pain of exclusion.

The image of her and Marco, sitting together at those times, the seductive concept this tiny infant could have been shared as a grandchild. She looked up and the spasm that crossed his face told her he was thinking the same. She tried to hold back the tears that prickled behind her eyes as her wounded heart gaped a little wider. 'You make friends easily.'

'But not keep them.' He tried to catch her eye again but this time she wouldn't let him.

She studied her granddaughter intently, checked the readings on the machines, examined the make and model of the open cot, looked any-where but at him. 'Perhaps they feel you cannot be relied on.'

He stepped closer and she could feel the hairs on her arms rise in anticipation. Couldn't help the deeper breath she took to inhale the subtle tang of his aftershave, the intrinsic masculine scent of Marco, that she would recognise anywhere. 'I would be here if you let me, Emily.' The words settled over her like a hug she couldn't touch.

Emily stood up. Picked up the bag she had for Annie. This was survival because if she didn't move now she'd throw herself onto his chest. 'It's called a short-term fix, Marco. The cure is worse than the disease.'

'How come Marco leaves every time you arrive to visit me?' Annie was straight to the point.

Emily tried not to wince. 'Do you think he does?' She knew he did. But that was what she'd asked for, space. It was hard enough without Annie on her case. Their bitter-sweet encounter in the NICU—bitter on her side and sweet on his—had almost done her in. The guilt for her harsh words ate away at her composure and she wasn't sure if she could take Annie's censure as well.

'I hadn't noticed.' Liar. Emily looked up. 'I thought Rosebud looked amazing this morning when I went across to the NICU after my shift.'

Emily adjusted some flowers in a vase as she smiled brightly. 'She even turned her head and opened her eyes for a few seconds.'

Instantly diverted Annie smiled and nodded. 'I know. She did it when I went down. Dr Teo is very happy with her progress and she's tolerating the tiny bit of milk from me down the tube really well.'

Emily's day brightened a little. 'That's wonderful, darling. A week being stable makes a big difference to a prem baby.'

Annie's eyes shone. 'Rodney's coming in early because they think we'll be able to have her naked against my skin for a while today.'

Emily smiled mistily. 'Kangaroo care. If it's after my sleep, can you ring me? I'd love to see her snuggle up to you.'

'You do look tired. Are you sleeping okay without me at home?'

'I'm fine.' She smiled and then nodded at

Annie's magnificent cleavage. 'I see your milk's come in.'

Annie poked her chest out and looked down with a smug smile. 'Did you know that my breasts make milk that suits the exact premature age my baby is?'

'Yep. Mother nature knows best.'

'That is so cool.' Then she fanned herself. 'Actually, my boobs are quite hot and sore but I'm telling myself I'd be more upset if they weren't working.'

Emily pulled a brown paper parcel from her bag. 'I have a present for you.'

'More presents?' Annie clapped her hands and Emily shook her head.

'You're spoilt but I think you'll appreciate these.' Emily laughed and tipped two opened disposable nappies out of her bag onto the bedside table and they rocked like little cradles. 'They're frozen. I poured some water on them and put them in the freezer and now you can open them out and wrap them around your breasts. It's just for the next twenty-four hours while you're engorged.'

'That's crazy.' Annie wasn't sure she was convinced this would be a good idea.

'Try them and see.' Emily helped Annie ease the crunchy nappies down into her bra and wrapped the cold netting around her hot breasts.

Her mouth pursed as she looked at her mother. 'Oh. Wow. That feels so-o-o good.'

'Excellent. And you just put them back into this plastic bag and pop them back in the freezer to re-freeze.'

'Awesome.'

'I bring the coolest gifts.' Mother and daughter grinned at each other.

Annie patted her chest and sighed blissfully. Then she sat up. 'Speaking of cool gifts, Marco brought me a card and more phone credit so I could ring Rodney whenever I wanted.'

Emily struggled to keep the smile on her face. 'That was nice of him.'

Annie's attention sharpened. 'Which brings me back to my original question. Have you two stopped seeing each other?'

Emily studied her fingers as she screwed up the brown paper bag on the bench. 'We were never really seeing each other. Did he say something?'

'Oh. Pleeease, Mum. You guys are hotter than my boobs for each other. And, no, he didn't say anything. He's a clam, like you.'

A clam. Where had she heard that? Emily drew a deep breath and faced her daughter with the truth. 'Look. He's going soon, Emily. You and Rosebud are my priorities.'

She slowed her words even more. 'I need to concentrate on what's important in my life and at this moment you and Rosebud top that list. I don't have space in my life for a doomed love affair.'

Annie wasn't having that. 'Why not?'

Emily closed her eyes and opened them again. 'Because I want to spend time with you. And my granddaughter. And be here for you both.'

Annie stared at her thoughtfully, chewed her lip, and finally sighed. 'I don't want you to take this the wrong way, Mum, but…' She reached out and took her mother's hand. Squeezed it. 'I'll always want your support and your love, it's just…maybe it's time you should think about your own life. Your own happiness.'

Annie drew a deep breath and began to speak faster, as if afraid her mother wouldn't understand if she didn't get the whole concept out before she was interrupted. 'Heck—even embrace being the wonderful, gorgeous woman you are and not just be a mum to me. Rodney's here for us, Mum. He's Rosebud's father. She has us and I have him. You deserve a man who cares too.'

Emily gulped, felt the sting of tears, and she forced them back with iron control, but she didn't know how she was going to get the words out. Her throat had closed and another dull ache opened in her chest. Imagine if she lost both Marco *and* Annie!

She squeezed the words out. 'I see.'

'No, you don't.' Annie climbed out from under the covers, took Emily's hand and pulled her down until they were sitting side by side on the edge of the bed.

'You look devastated. Don't be. You're my mum, my hero, for goodness' sake, there is nobody in this world who can do what you do, make things happen like you can.' Annie squeezed her hand again. 'You're amazing.'

Annie shrugged. Patted her mother's hand like she was the mentor here. 'I just think you might have found an awesome guy who actually has an inkling how cool you really are, and you're beating him off with a stick.'

Annie hugged her mother carefully, and the ice in her bra crackled between them, until Emily gave a watery smile. 'Please don't be hurt because I'm actually thinking of you for a change.'

A lone tear trickled annoyingly down her cheek and Emily brushed it away impatiently. Tried to take in her daughter's words and the sense behind them, but the flicker of fear hovered in her throat. What if she did lose both of them? And it was already too late for Marco. 'But he's going.'

Annie snorted and for a moment there she sounded like Gran. 'Well, for goodness' sake, do something about that. If anybody can, you're the one.' She looked at her mother. 'But you'd better go home and go to bed for a couple of hours before you take on the weekend. You look tired. We have the baby shower tomorrow afternoon in the NICU.'

It was only an afternoon tea but Rosebud nearly missed it. Her see-through skin tinged yellow like a baby banana with jaundice. Not surprising really. Her tiny liver was so immature it couldn't handle the breaking down of her unneeded blood cells now that she was in the outside world.

It just meant Rosebud couldn't watch with her painted blindfold sunglasses on as she lay under phototherapy. But the air was warm, and love and caring drifted her way from her family and their friends, and the purple light that shone on her was doing the job her liver couldn't.

'Never mind,' Rodney said. 'She sleeps a lot anyway, like her mother.' And everyone smiled.

The original baby shower had been planned for today at Emily and Annie's home.

For obvious reasons that wasn't possible but the NICU girls who'd helped look after Annie during those first few difficult weeks sixteen years ago had decided Annie's own daughter held a special place in their hearts and they wanted to be a part of Rosebud's baby shower.

Along with the fact that most of the guest list worked in the hospital, it was a crowded but well-behaved affair.

Rodney brought one friend, Jack, a big, blond, punk-haired and pierced bouncer, who turned out to be a favourite once they could stop him washing his hands and making sure he was clean enough to come in.

Jack kept punching Rodney in the shoulder and telling him, 'You're so lucky, man.' And Rodney just nodded and glowed and hugged Annie.

Rodney had brought Annie a gift-wrapped box with tiny rosebud earrings and for his daughter the smallest bracelet with her name engraved on it and a little pink rabbit.

Emily had found the softest little pink lace cap for Rosebud to wear. She would have liked to show it to Marco but he wasn't there. She'd have liked to show Marco lots of things but she had driven him away. Teo and Zoe brought exquisite tiny doll's clothes and Lily and Luke brought a doll to dress up after Rosebud grew out of them.

Even Finn and Evie showed and chose a magnificent pink shawl to take Rosebud home in when the time came.

Annie floated graciously around, thanking people.

Emily passed around fairy bread and tiny scones and jam and cream and held onto her pride for the maturity of her own daughter while she kept the tears at the back of her throat.

And Marco should be here. Even Annie had commented sadly that he must be very busy.

Emily knew their last conversation had driven him away. Not surprisingly.

She couldn't deny his absence left an aching sense of loss she hoped nobody else saw, and she only had herself to blame.

All the while Rosebud slept on in her little sun bed, oblivious to the subdued good wishes from her departing guests.

When all was eaten, when presents were stored and everyone but the NICU staff had drifted away, Emily sat in the chair beside her grand-daughter. Annie had gone out for the afternoon with Rodney instead of going back to the ac-commodation put aside for mothers with sick babies, so Emily was alone.

She gazed unseeingly at the open crib, tried to let the beeps of the machines wash over her, but seemed only able to replay her conversation with Marco from the previous morning.

Emily turned her head and stared with stinging eyes at the little determined chin that poked out from under the eye protection. 'You're so like your mother.'

Her daughter's words circled around and around in her head. Even Annie's words in Marco's office came back to haunt her. Yes—she had tried to be everything for Annie. Had chosen the night shift so nobody could say she was leaving her baby for her gran to rear. Had pushed any thought of a relationship away because someone might say—or she might feel—she wasn't doing the job well enough. Perhaps it hadn't been those few men who had been lacking—but her. She just didn't have what it took for a man to fight for her. Or was it she that lacked the fight?

Footsteps and then Marco's voice came from behind her as his hand rested lightly on her shoulder. 'Did you have a nice party?'

She put her fingers up and over his hand. Felt the strength in those fingers that could be so gentle. Fingers that could caress her so eloquently they almost sang against her skin. So he had come. The overwhelming relief and comfort made her shoulders drop. Without turning, she said, 'Annie was sorry you couldn't make it.'

His hand tightened. 'Only Annie?'

CHAPTER THIRTEEN

'RODNEY missed you too,' Emily said, with the first tinge of humour she'd felt all day.

'Ah, my friend Rodney.' He stood behind her for a moment longer and then lifted his hand. She missed it already but he'd stepped away to bring a chair.

'May I?' When she nodded he placed it beside her so that they both faced Rosebud's open crib. 'You are very good to Rodney.'

Was she? 'Rodney is very good with Annie. If he wasn't, it would be a different story.'

'I can see that.' He smiled and she had to smile back because they both knew how protective she was of her daughter. 'But you do not hold his family history against him.'

She heard the dark taste of bitterness in his voice. Frowned at it as she tried to imagine where it had come from. 'Why would I do that?'

'Forgive me.' He shrugged. 'The first day you met Rodney, I too saw him, and overheard Annie tell you his brother was in jail. Your distress was clear.'

Emily had no idea where he was a going with this but something warned her that was very important to Marco and therefore it was important to her.

She needed to be careful how she answered so she watched his face. Tried not to be distracted by how much she enjoyed just looking at him. 'That's got nothing to do with Rodney.'

He shrugged. 'How is this nothing to do with Rodney?'

'Why would it be? I didn't ask him to, but he explained how his brother became involved in a bad crowd, and now pays the price for that. I try to take people how I find them. Rodney is not the one in trouble and cannot be held accountable. He has a good heart and genuinely loves Annie and Rosebud.'

She shrugged. 'Still, they are very young and it will be hard to grow up at the same pace from this age—but that's for them to decide and discover for themselves.'

He raised his brows and she could see that he was surprised. 'So you expect them to move in together?'

She supposed that was liberal from an Italian male's point of view. 'I haven't come to that conclusion yet. Maybe not for a long time. But Rodney doesn't have a satisfactory place to stay and he wants to carry some of the load in caring for Rosebud when she comes home. We'll see. Maybe he'll stay weekends.'

'You are a very understanding person.'

Except to him. He should know she could be better at that. 'I'd be the pot calling the kettle black.'

He frowned. 'This is like fishing?'

'A colloquialism. Yes.' She smiled. 'I will miss you. And I'm sorry I pushed you away the other day.' There, she'd said it. She went on in a bright little voice that only just cracked. 'So, when do you leave?'

Marco heard the tiny element of distress and told himself he'd imagined it. 'Tomorrow. I have come to say goodbye.'

'Tomorrow.' More brightness. 'You didn't give yourself much down time to see Sydney.'

He glanced across at Rosebud. 'I've seen the important parts.' Glanced back at her and smiled and something in his expression made her eyes sting with emotion. 'I have been on the important rides.'

She turned to face him. Touched his sleeve and tried to smile. 'We had a lovely time. Thank you.'

So it ended, Marco thought. He looked across at her. Held his hand back forcibly so that he didn't caress her hair or run his finger down her cheek despite the overwhelming urge to do so. 'I will miss everyone here.' He was surprised how much. This was what happened when you opened your heart. The pain soaked in. As he deserved.

'And we will miss you.'

Perhaps they would. For a brief while until he was forgotten. He glanced at the baby girl with her sunglasses on. He would miss seeing Rosebud grow stronger, grow more alert and active, start to make noises. Cry louder. Demand food. Recognise her mother. Recognise her grandmother.

The impact of his next thought vibrated in his head. Now this tiny infant would never recognise him. He had to leave this woman and this baby and this family, and that tore his heart into tiny strips.

He stood up. Lifted his chair and put it against the wall and then he came back to her for the last time. 'Goodbye, Emily.'

Emerrrlee! Emily watched him turn, take two steps. Had she not thought Marco was worth the same fighting spirit she'd always found for Annie? Was the chance of happiness with Marco and perhaps his happiness with her as well at stake and she was willing to let him fly away? For ever?

'Marco?'

He stopped and she stood and crossed the space to him. 'Why do you have to go?'

He squared his shoulders and did not meet her eyes. 'Because that is what I do.'

She wanted him to look at her. 'Why?'

'Because I learnt this during my childhood.'

Even with his chin averted she saw the pain cross his face. Felt his anguish. She so wanted to understand.

He went on. 'My childhood was a series of up-rootings in the night. My earliest memories of hurriedly dressing, told to be silent, hide before questions were asked. Such memories burn holes in the psyche that I have not yet filled. Now my parents are dead and at most I have vowed never to return to the place I felt so branded by disgust. As a boy I learnt to accept that I am not good enough for any parent's daughter.' He lifted his head. 'Not good enough for you.'

No. That wasn't how she wanted him to leave. 'I think you're amazing!'

'Ah. The amazing Dr D'Arvello. My work is good.' Simple truth. 'You do not know of my family.'

She reached out and touched his sleeve. Felt

the tension in his shoulder even through the fabric.

Marco wanted to squeeze her hand against his arm with his fingers so that she was welded to him. So he couldn't lose her. He could not believe he had told her some of his past. Never had this happened with a woman.

'Your family do not matter to me.' He heard her words but did not believe them. She went on. 'I know about you. The Marco we all care about. Of how much my family love you. Of your kindness and your strength and your amazing heart.'

Her words unmanned him. He shook his head. She had no concept. Could not know. 'My father.'

She lifted her fingers and stopped his words at his lips. Such gentle insistence. 'And you felt tainted by him. Like Rodney did.' Her words seeped into the wall he had guarded for all these years. Washed away the mud that had stuck to him for so long. Exposed his need to the day-light of her caring.

He hadn't thought of it like that but, yes, and the voice inside his head insisted, she had accepted Rodney for who he was.

She went on in that calm and almost steady voice, 'So if you didn't seek a relationship, nobody could say no?' She gave a strangled laugh. 'Imagine that. You and I are not dissimilar, you know.'

And the light cracked through like the peep of sunlight through one broken slat of a fastened shutter.

She felt that way too? Was this why no man had carried her off?

She lifted her chin high. Drew a breath and stared up into his eyes, and he could not look away, could feel the physical embrace though she wasn't touching him, such intimate connection as he stared into the depth of his Emily's green soul.

'I wish you could stay. Please don't go.' He shook his head and he saw she thought he was saying no. But it was in wonder of this woman. How did she have that strength? Risk all and stand before him so resolutely? Ask the question he hadn't realised he'd longed to hear. How could he have arrived at this moment in life and suddenly seen the light?

A light that blinded him. The light that was Emily.

'And if I stayed, would you share yourself with me? Share your family? Your heart?' He grinned and suddenly joy bubbled from within. Swept away the years of bitterness and fizzed in his bloodstream. 'Share your house?'

She pretended to frown at him but he was not fooled, could see a little of that joy in her face too now. 'That would depend on how long you were staying.'

'Ah,' he teased. 'That would depend on how long you would have me.'

She smiled slowly, with such tenderness and warmth he blinked. 'A long, long time.'

A sudden vision of her grandfather's family home. Renovations. Perhaps even extensions for all the children or grandchildren they would have. Little girls and boys running on the freshly mown grass. Perhaps another baby shower with tents and tiny pink cakes and women with sunshades all watching the children and the boats on the harbour. And Emily. Always Emily. 'Then in that case I have seen a house I wish to buy.'

She frowned. 'You've been looking at houses?'

'I didn't mean to.' He could do nothing but smile at her. Loving her confusion, loving her bravery, loving her. 'Someone I know has a house near you and I have grown very fond of your ferries and your harbour. And if I bought it, restored it to its former glory, perhaps you would move there with me. Make a gate in the side fence to join your grandmother's house. We would know our neighbours very well.' He could see Annie swinging Rosebud as she came through the gate to visit her mother. His daughter, his granddaughter, his family.

Emily's nerves were settling. She didn't know what he was talking about but there were more important things going on here than houses.

She couldn't believe she'd dared to ask. Dared to dream and give that dream a chance. Fought for him and very possibly, judging by the adoring look on his face, perhaps won. 'Do you think you'd be able to find work?' she teased.

'I am sure.' He smiled that smile that lifted her feet off the ground then whispered almost to himself, 'Never did I think I would say these words.'

He glanced at Rosebud, almost as if to ask permission, then back at Emily. Stared into her eyes and the love that shone from his face took her breath away. *'Amore mio, per favour, sposami.'* Then more strongly, again in English, as if something had been set free with the words in his native tongue. 'My love. Please. Be my wife.'

Emily stared into his beloved face. His wife! This man who had turned her life upside down, whose strength and kindness and skills had saved her family, and whose passion and warmth and caring had saved her.

She reached up, cradled his face and gently kissed his lips. 'With all my heart, my love.'

Three months later, at sunset, a three-masted brig drifted away from the wharf at Darling Harbour.

It seemed the captain was a real captain and

could marry those aboard his ship once outside the heads.

At the bow of the ship, with his hands clenched behind his back, a tall, dark man stood anxiously, magnificently dressed in coat and tails, and waited for the ship to sail out to sea.

Marco drew in the salt-laden air and savoured the breeze at his back as he stared down the length of the ship, past the guests seated on the chairs arranged under the masts, all craning for a glimpse of Emily. His life had changed so much in the last precious months and it was all because of the woman he waited for.

As they'd arrived for the wedding Emily had decided each guest should be given a wristband that entitled them to free rides for the rest of the night at Luna Park after the wedding reception. They wanted to share their love and excitement with all of their friends, and what better way than at a funfair?

At the stern of the ship the bride, in an exquisite sixty-year-old lace wedding dress, with her beautiful daughter as her bridesmaid, stood framed against the sunset as the ship passed under the Sydney Harbour Bridge under sail.

Annie held Emily's posy of pale pink rosebuds, in honour of the bride's granddaughter, too young to be flower girl but old enough to be held by her father as they waited in readiness for the ceremony.

The bride's hands shook slightly as she imagined the time when she would walk the length of the ship and bind herself for ever to the man she loved, and her fingers shook so much that her engagement rings, one old that had belonged to her grandmother and the new, a magnificent emerald, caught every ray of light from the pinkening sky.

Finally it was time. The music drifted towards her on the afternoon breeze and Annie leaned across and kissed her mother's cheek. 'You look beautiful. Good luck.' She handed her the posy.

'Good luck?' Emily laughed and her fingers relaxed as the movement stilled. She lifted her face to the breeze. 'I don't need luck. I have Marco!'

* * * * *

Mills & Boon® Large Print Medical

February

SYDNEY HARBOUR HOSPITAL: AVA'S RE-AWAKENING	Carol Marinelli
HOW TO MEND A BROKEN HEART	Amy Andrews
FALLING FOR DR FEARLESS	Lucy Clark
THE NURSE HE SHOULDN'T NOTICE	Susan Carlisle
EVERY BOY'S DREAM DAD	Sue MacKay
RETURN OF THE REBEL SURGEON	Connie Cox

March

HER MOTHERHOOD WISH	Anne Fraser
A BOND BETWEEN STRANGERS	Scarlet Wilson
ONCE A PLAYBOY…	Kate Hardy
CHALLENGING THE NURSE'S RULES	Janice Lynn
THE SHEIKH AND THE SURROGATE MUM	Meredith Webber
TAMED BY HER BROODING BOSS	Joanna Neil

April

A SOCIALITE'S CHRISTMAS WISH	Lucy Clark
REDEEMING DR RICCARDI	Leah Martyn
THE FAMILY WHO MADE HIM WHOLE	Jennifer Taylor
THE DOCTOR MEETS HER MATCH	Annie Claydon
THE DOCTOR'S LOST-AND-FOUND HEART	Dianne Drake
THE MAN WHO WOULDN'T MARRY	Tina Beckett

Mills & Boon® Large Print Medical

May

MAYBE THIS CHRISTMAS…?	Alison Roberts
A DOCTOR, A FLING & A WEDDING RING	Fiona McArthur
DR CHANDLER'S SLEEPING BEAUTY	Melanie Milburne
HER CHRISTMAS EVE DIAMOND	Scarlet Wilson
NEWBORN BABY FOR CHRISTMAS	Fiona Lowe
THE WAR HERO'S LOCKED-AWAY HEART	Louisa George

June

FROM CHRISTMAS TO ETERNITY	Caroline Anderson
HER LITTLE SPANISH SECRET	Laura Iding
CHRISTMAS WITH DR DELICIOUS	Sue MacKay
ONE NIGHT THAT CHANGED EVERYTHING	Tina Beckett
CHRISTMAS WHERE SHE BELONGS	Meredith Webber
HIS BRIDE IN PARADISE	Joanna Neil

July

THE SURGEON'S DOORSTEP BABY	Marion Lennox
DARE SHE DREAM OF FOREVER?	Lucy Clark
CRAVING HER SOLDIER'S TOUCH	Wendy S. Marcus
SECRETS OF A SHY SOCIALITE	Wendy S. Marcus
BREAKING THE PLAYBOY'S RULES	Emily Forbes
HOT-SHOT DOC COMES TO TOWN	Susan Carlisle